THE
TRUTH
APP

THE TRUTH APP

LIARS BOOK 1

Jack Heath

SIMON & SCHUSTER BFYR

NEW YORK LONDON TORONTO SYDNEY NEW DELHI

SIMON & SCHUSTER BFYR

An imprint of Simon & Schuster Children's Publishing Division
1230 Avenue of the Americas, New York, New York 10020
This book is a work of fiction. Any references to historical events, real people, or
real places are used fictitiously. Other names, characters, places, and events are
products of the author's imagination, and any resemblance to actual events or
places or persons, living or dead, is entirely coincidental.
Text copyright © 2018 by Jack Heath
Originally published in Australia in 2018 by Scholastic Australia Pty Limited
This edition published under license from Scholastic Australia Pty Limited
All rights reserved, including the right of reproduction in whole
or in part in any form.
SIMON & SCHUSTER BFYR is a trademark of Simon & Schuster, Inc.
For information about special discounts for bulk purchases, please contact Simon &
Schuster Special Sales at 1-866-506-1949 or business@simonandschuster.com.
The Simon & Schuster Speakers Bureau can bring authors to your live event.
For more information or to book an event, contact the Simon & Schuster Speakers
Bureau at 1-866-248-3049 or visit our website at www.simonspeakers.com.
Jacket design by Greg Stadnyk
Interior design by Hilary Zarycky
The text for this book was set in New Caledonia.
Manufactured in the United States of America
2 4 6 8 10 9 7 5 3
Library of Congress Cataloging-in-Publication Data
Names: Heath, Jack, 1986– author.
Title: The Truth app / Jack Heath.
Description: First US edition. | New York : SSBFYR, 2020. | Series: Liars ; 1
| "Originally published in Australia in 2018 by Scholastic
Australia"—Copyright page. | Summary: High schooler Jarli Durras becomes an
overnight celebrity after creating an app that can tell when a person
is lying, but his fame soon turns dangerous when a secret network of
criminals adds Jarli to its hit list.
Identifiers: LCCN 2018058537|
ISBN 9781534449862 (hardcover) | ISBN 9781534449886 (eBook)
Subjects: | CYAC: Application software—Fiction. | Fame—Fiction. | Honesty—
Fiction. | Secrets—Fiction. | Criminals—Fiction. | Computer crimes—Fiction.
Classification: LCC PZ7.H3478 Tr 2020 | DDC [Fic]—dc23
LC record available at https://lccn.loc.gov/2018058537

For the real Ashley Arthur, friend indeed

PART ONE: ASSASSIN

Hey, nerds!

I've been making a lie detector app. It uses the speech recognition code that Randall787 posted last week (thanks, Randy!) to understand what someone is saying, then compares that to a list of evasive phrases. It also uses guitar-tuning software to see if someone's voice is suspiciously high (which might mean they're nervous), and a face-reader plug-in to see if it looks like the person is thinking too hard (lying takes more concentration than telling the truth).

Can you guys help me test it? Download link is below.
truthapp-1.1.zip

Thanks,
JarJarStinks05

—From the documentation for Truth, *version 1.1*

High-Speed Collision

There was no warning at all. Just a flicker in the corner of Jarli's eye.

He turned his head just in time to see the brown truck roaring toward Dad's side of the car. Jarli opened his mouth to scream—

Smash! The impact threw him sideways. The seat belt jerked tight across his chest, crushing his ribs. He couldn't get any air into his lungs. Half the car crumpled in toward Dad, who had let go of the steering wheel and thrown his arms up to protect his face.

"Daaaaaaad!" The screech of tearing metal drowned out Jarli's voice. The sound burned through his eardrums and sank deep into his skull. The windows dissolved into tiny cubes of shatterproof glass that filled the air like hail, stinging his cheeks. He squeezed his eyes shut.

A few moments later everything was still. The echoes of screeching tires died away. The smell of melted rubber scorched the back of Jarli's throat.

The truck started to reverse, taking Dad's door with it. The window frame was tangled around the truck's chrome bull bar. The hinges screeched and snapped, leaving the driver's side of the car ripped open. The truck's headlights stunned Jarli. They seemed as bright as twin suns.

The engine whined as the truck backed away.

"Dad?" Jarli croaked. He could barely hear his own voice over the ringing in his ears.

Dad turned his head like it weighed a ton, his curly hair glued to his forehead with sweat.

". . . ?" Dad asked.

"What?" Jarli wiggled his jaw, trying to fix his ears.

". . . okay?" Dad said again.

Jarli nodded, sending a jab of pain up his neck. "I think I'm all right. Are you—"

Vvvvvrooom! An engine snarled. Jarli looked over and saw the brown truck zooming toward the car again. He got a split-second view of an old man with thick black glasses and a baseball cap, gloved hands gripping the steering wheel. Suddenly Jarli realized: This crash was not an accident.

The old man in the truck was attacking them.

"Watch out!" Jarli screamed.

Dad slammed his foot down on the accelerator. The wrecked car lurched forward, bent wheels grinding. Too slow.

The speeding truck smashed into the rear corner of the car, sending it into a spin. The world outside the windows rushed past. The neon vacancy sign outside Kelton's motel flew across Jarli's field of view twice. He felt like he might throw up.

Clang! The car hit a streetlight and stopped spinning. Jarli slumped back into his seat, too dizzy to move. The streetlight leaned over and then paused, as though deciding whether to fall. It didn't, but the bulb dropped out of it and shattered against the road like a water balloon. The street was plunged into darkness.

Jarli fumbled with his seat belt, hands shaking. He stabbed the orange button with his thumb until the buckle popped out. Then he shoved the door open and tumbled out onto the road. "He's trying to kill us!" he cried, scrambling to his feet. "Run!" Dizzy and sore, Jarli ran on wobbling legs past the dead streetlight, past the motel with its darkened windows, past the trash cans—

And then he realized Dad wasn't with him.

He turned to look back. The wrecked car was deep in shadow, but Jarli could see Dad's outline. He was slumped in the driver's seat. The second impact had knocked him out. Or worse.

Heart pounding, Jarli looked around for help. He couldn't see anyone. No police, no other vehicles, no pedestrians. Another quiet night in Kelton. But he could hear the truck's motor, idling somewhere in the gloom, headlights off. The old man could ram the car again at any moment. And Dad was a sitting duck.

Jarli sprinted back to the car. As he got closer, he saw that an airbag had exploded out of the steering wheel. Dad's face was buried in the white fabric.

"Dad!" Jarli screamed. "Wake up!"

He grabbed his father's shoulders and pulled him backward, leaving a smudge of blood on the airbag. There was a deep cut across the bridge of Dad's nose and his cheekbone had turned a mottled purple. His eyes were closed.

Tires crunched. An engine grumbled. The truck was coming back.

Frantic, Jarli reached over, unbuckled Dad's seat belt, and tried to drag him out of the car. But Jarli was still dizzy, and Dad was too heavy. Jarli fell back and Dad landed on him, crushing Jarli's legs against the road.

Headlights swept across them. The truck was back!

Dad felt like a bag of bricks. Jarli couldn't roll him off.

He braced himself as the headlights got closer.

Something Wrong

I t was the word "secrets" that got Anya's attention.

"You always keep secrets from *me*."

Anya shifted in her chair to glance sideways at the boy who had spoken. He was a year or two younger than her, with curly black hair and a fidgety kind of walk. Anya had never talked to him, but there were only two hundred kids at Kelton High School, so she had seen him around. His name wasn't Charlie—it was something odd, like Chardi, or Jarli.

Mr. Lang droned on and on, talking to her mother. Anya's attention remained focused on the boy. He was walking toward the exit with his father, who looked like a bigger version of him, but with some gray stubble and a cleaner T-shirt. They had just finished their meeting with Mr. Kendrick, who was quietly fuming at a small desk behind them.

The boy and his dad both looked frustrated—like almost everyone else in the room. It was parent-teacher night.

"I do not," the father was saying.

"Then how come you won't let me use your computer?"

"Because—"

"And the phone calls you make at night. I can hear you through the wall."

"Keep your voice down." The father cast an anxious glance around the gym.

Anya quickly looked away, but kept listening.

"Don't change the subject," the father continued. "Yes, I keep aspects of my work confidential. Most professionals do. That's completely different from you hacking into your teacher's e-mails."

"It's not like I read any of them."

"Oh, is that right?"

"You don't believe me?" The boy sounded offended.

Anya was surprised. She hadn't picked him as a rebel. Whenever she was transferred to a new school in a new town, the first thing she did was identify the disobedient kids, and steer clear. No judgment—she just didn't want teachers to assume things about her because of who she sat with. She'd gotten pretty good at spotting the disrupters by their clothes, their hair, and the way they talked . . .

Or didn't talk. Nearby, a group of students were waiting to be eviscerated by their teachers. Doug Hennessey was at the front of the line, next to a woman who was probably his mother. Doug was lanky and gaunt with blond hair smeared sideways across his scalp. Anya had never heard him say a single word. He was a new student, like her, but he always looked either gloomy or angry. She avoided him at all costs.

"Just be normal," Doug's mother was saying. "Okay? It's not that hard."

Doug didn't answer her. He was practically glowing with fury, all aimed at Jarli/Chardi. Anya wondered what he'd done to make Doug mad.

"Anya."

Anya turned. Her mother and Mr. Lang were staring at her.

"You're not paying attention," her mother said.

This was not true. Anya always paid attention. She sometimes thought she was the only person in Kelton who did. No one else seemed to notice the strange vibe here. It was a town of fewer than a thousand people, hundreds of miles from anywhere, and yet unfamiliar faces showed up all the time. Locals often left town without explanation. Buildings that were supposedly abandoned had guards around the clock. And then there was that weird rich guy up in the hills, piloting his drones every day.

"I'm listening." Anya turned back to Mr. Lang. "You were saying that my essay about copyright lacked a strong conclusion."

Lang cleared his throat. "Uh, yes. The essay—"

"Because it's a complex issue, with no clear answer."

"Anya," her mother said. "Don't interrupt."

"The essay was supposed to support one side or the other." Lang talked slowly, as though she was stupid. "That was the assignment—to argue a position."

"To lie," Anya said.

Lang blinked his watery eyes.

"It's not lying," her mother said patiently. "It's called persuasive writing."

"To say something I don't believe to be true," Anya said, "is the definition of lying."

Lang sighed. "In any case, the research was excellent, especially for a student studying English as a second language. Once again, Anya received the top mark for her class."

"Thank you, Mr. Lang," Anya said. She stood, and her mother reluctantly did too.

Then Anya felt the energy in the room shift. Silence fell.

She turned around. A woman had entered the gymnasium. She had a mane of shiny chestnut hair, ironed clothes—unheard of in Kelton—and lipstick as red as blood. She held a phone that had a spongy black microphone plugged into it.

"Is that Dana Reynolds?" someone whispered.

The name jogged Anya's memory. The woman was a news reporter from the city. She looked different on TV. Taller, somehow, even though she was usually sitting down.

"Jarli Durras?" Reynolds called out.

There was a pause. Anya looked around, but Jarli was gone.

"He just left," Anya said.

Reynolds's clear green eyes settled on Anya. "Are you a friend of his?" she asked.

"No," Anya said.

The woman exhaled through her perfect teeth.

"I am," another girl offered. "Is this about the app?"

The girl had a nose stud and a punky sort of haircut, long on one side and shaved on the other. She was leaning on crutches. Anya didn't know her name.

Reynolds hurried over to her. "Perfect. What's your name, sweetheart?"

"Bess."

Anya wanted to hear more, but her mother grabbed her arm. "Come, Anya."

As her mother led her out of the gym, Anya watched from the corner of her eye as Reynolds began to quiz Bess.

The fresh air outside was a relief. The gym didn't have air-conditioning. Anya took boxing lessons there on Thursdays and she was always amazed by how hot it was, even at night.

On the other side of the parking lot, Jarli and his father were clambering into a hybrid car, still arguing. Reynolds must have walked right past him. Maybe she didn't know what he looked like.

An old man with black-rimmed glasses sat in a brown truck not far away. Waiting for his grandchildren to finish up inside, maybe. But after a few seconds he started his engine and drove out of the lot, following Jarli's hybrid. Weird.

"So," Anya's mother said. "Room for improvement."

"Lang just said I was at the top of my class. Again."

"A small class. In a *rural* school."

Anya winced. Harsh.

"It doesn't matter how you compare to the other students," her mother said, for what had to be the hundredth time. "What matters is how you compare to your own potential. And I know you can do better."

"Yes, Mother," Anya said. She remembered what Doug's mother had told him: *Just be normal.* Why weren't her own parents ever satisfied with that?

She climbed into the four-wheel drive and her mother started the engine. On their way out of the parking lot, they drove past a polished sports car that probably belonged to Dana Reynolds. Anya wondered why she wanted to talk to Jarli. What was the app that Bess had mentioned?

Just another mystery, in a town full of them.

Anya lived on the western edge of Kelton—which wasn't far from the eastern edge. They would be home in ten minutes. Anya rolled down the window, feeling the wind on her face. She closed her eyes and rested her head against the seat. Maybe she could go for a run when she got home. Spy on the neighbors. Unravel some of Kelton's secrets.

"What the . . ."

Anya opened her eyes. On the road ahead of them a wrecked car was pressed against a leaning streetlight. The car was so smashed up that it took her a minute to recognize Jarli's hybrid.

Like a Ghost

The truck stopped, brakes squeaking.

Jarli sheltered his eyes from the light as the driver got out. It wasn't the old man with the thick black glasses. It was a middle-aged woman with striped trousers and blond hair held back by a gray headband. She looked horrified. As Jarli's eyes adjusted, he saw that her vehicle wasn't a truck—it was a mud-spattered four-wheel drive.

"What happened?" the woman gasped.

"Watch out!" Jarli said. "There's this guy—this crazy guy in a big truck. He tried to kill us!"

The woman looked around. "What truck?"

Jarli turned his head. He couldn't see it from here, and he couldn't move to get a better look. Dad was still squashing his legs.

A teenage girl got out of the four-wheel drive. She wore black jeans and a black T-shirt with a logo too faded to read. Jarli recognized her from school—she was new, and a couple of years older than him.

"Anya!" the woman said. "Stay in the car."

Ignoring her mother, Anya ran over to Jarli. Her tattered sneakers crunched over the broken glass surrounding the wrecked hybrid.

"Are you hurt?" she asked. Her voice was deeper than Jarli had expected, with an accent of some kind. At school, Jarli had never heard her speak.

"My dad won't wake up," Jarli said. His throat felt swollen, like he was having an allergic reaction to the words. "Please. You gotta help him."

Anya's mother was on the phone. "Ambulance," she said. Her accent was stronger than her daughter's. "There has been a car accident."

"Not an accident," Jarli croaked. "The old man crashed into us on purpose."

"We are on Juniper Street," the woman continued, ignoring him. "The nearest intersection is . . ." She turned around a few times and then gave up. "I don't know. We are next to the Kelton Motor Inn. Do you know where that is?"

Anya crouched down next to Jarli and grabbed Dad's shoulder. "Let's roll him off you," she said. "You push, and I will pull. Okay?"

"Okay."

"One, two, three!"

Jarli pushed Dad from underneath as Anya heaved him off. She held the back of his head so it didn't hit the road.

Then she poked a finger under his jaw, checking his pulse. Jarli was amazed at how calm she seemed.

"What is his name?" she asked.

"Glen," Jarli said. "Glen Durras."

"Hey, Glen! Can you hear me, Glen?"

"Come quick," Anya's mother was saying into the phone.

Jarli stood and looked around for the truck. The street was still deserted. There was only one set of skid marks on the road. They led to Dad's car and the damaged streetlight. It looked like Dad had lost control, slammed on the brakes, and hit the streetlight. It was as though the truck had never existed. The husk of the ripped-out car door lay abandoned, like driftwood, a few yards away.

"Glen," Anya said again. "Come on. Wake up."

Dad groaned.

"Dad!" Jarli cried. He went to hug Dad, but Anya held him back.

"Just a minute," she said. "Give him some air."

"What was . . ." Dad began. His eyelids fluttered. "Who . . ."

"The ambulance is coming," Jarli said. "Don't move, okay?"

Dad tried to nod, but groaned in pain. He must have hurt his head or his neck.

"Thank you," Jarli told Anya.

She shrugged. "I did not really do anything."

"Jarli," Dad mumbled. But his eyes were closed. It was like he was talking in his sleep.

"I'm here," Jarli said, squeezing Dad's shoulder.

"The laptop," Dad said. "Don't let them . . ."

It was typical of Dad to be worried about his laptop, even at a time like this.

"Mum will take care of your laptop." Jarli squeezed Dad's hand. "Just chill."

Dad opened his eyes and tried to sit up. Anya put a hand on his arm. "Try not to move," she said.

Dad didn't seem to hear her. He was looking around at the road and the smashed car, but it was as though he was seeing something else. His wounded face was a terrible sight. He didn't even look like Dad anymore.

"Viper," he whispered.

"It's okay," Jarli said. Dad had always been sensible and reliable. It was scary to see him talking nonsense like this. What if the crash had damaged his brain?

A siren was getting closer. Jarli turned to Anya's mother. "Did you call the police?"

"The ambulance, yes," she said, putting her phone back in her handbag.

"No. We need the police. Someone tried to kill us."

She frowned. "It looks like it was just an accident. Do not worry."

But Anya's eyes narrowed. "Why would someone try to kill you?" she asked.

"I have no idea."

"Do you have any enemies?"

Jarli half laughed. But Anya looked dead serious.

"Well, my history teacher hates me," Jarli said. "But I'm pretty sure it wasn't him behind the wheel."

"So you actually saw the driver?"

"Anya," her mother warned.

"Yeah," Jarli said. "For a second. He was old—and he was wearing glasses."

He realized as he said this that it wasn't much to go on. He could hear the ambulance siren getting louder and louder.

"Glasses with black frames?" Anya asked. "Was he driving a brown truck?"

Jarli stared. "How do you know that?"

"Anya," her mother warned, "this is not the time."

Anya ignored her. "Do you have a dash cam?"

"No," Jarli said. Dad hadn't wanted a camera in the car. He worried that it could be used to spy on him. Dad could be kind of paranoid.

Anya looked surprised. "In Russia, everyone has a dash cam."

So that was where Anya was from. "Nothing happens in Kelton," Jarli said defensively. "There'd be nothing to record."

Anya looked at the wrecked car. "So I see."

"Hide it," Dad muttered. "Gotta hide it."

An ambulance appeared at the far end of the street, lights flashing, engine rumbling. Anya's mother waved her arms at it. "Over here!"

The ambulance switched off its siren and stopped next to the ruined car. Two paramedics leaped out—a man and a woman. The man went around the back to get a stretcher while the woman ran over to Jarli's dad. She wore dark overalls and had a stethoscope around her neck. A radio was attached to her hip.

"Who was in the car?" she asked. Like Anya, she talked quickly but calmly.

"Me and my dad," Jarli said. "He's talking, but he's not making sense. His name is Glen Durras."

"You're not hurt?"

"No."

The paramedic shone a small flashlight into Dad's eyes. "Glen? Can you hear me?"

Dad blinked. "Who are you?" he asked. "What do you want?"

"I'm a paramedic," the woman said. "My name is Susan. I'm here to help you, okay? Are you in pain?"

Dad shook his head vigorously, and then pressed his hands to his temples.

"We're going to take you to hospital now, okay?" Susan said.

The male paramedic rolled the stretcher over and lowered it to the ground beside Dad. "What do we have?" he asked.

Susan kept her voice low, but Jarli heard what she said. "Possible bleeding in the brain."

"This corner is a death trap," the male paramedic said. His name badge read: TYSON. "That's the third accident here this year."

"It wasn't an accident," Jarli said again. "Is Dad going to be okay?"

Susan helped Tyson lift Dad onto the stretcher. "Is there someone you can call?" she asked Jarli. "Your mum, maybe?"

Mum. What would Jarli tell Mum? She was going to freak out.

Jarli got out his phone. It was in airplane mode—he hadn't been allowed to use it at the parent-teacher meeting. As Jarli reconnected it to the network, his *Truth* app popped up on the screen. He had been testing it before the meeting. The app was supposed to be able to tell if people were lying, but he was still working out the bugs.

He minimized it so he could call Mum. "What should I say?"

"Tell her to meet you at the hospital," Susan said. "You can ride with us. We'll need to examine you as well." She rolled Dad's stretcher over to the ambulance and Tyson helped her slide it into the back.

"Let us know what happens," Anya said. "Okay?"

"Okay. Thanks." Jarli turned back to the paramedics. "Is Dad going to be all right?" he asked again.

"I'm sure he'll be fine," Susan said.

Jarli's phone beeped and the screen flashed red. A warning message came up: *Lie.*

Going Viral

The inside of the ambulance was like a spaceship, or maybe a submarine—tiny, but packed with stuff. There were bottles of disinfectant, burn gel, hand sanitizer, water, juice, and other liquids Jarli didn't recognize. A bandage roll as big as a bike tire was mounted on the wall next to a pair of defibrillator paddles. A bin was marked: HAZARDOUS WASTE. A mini fridge was stocked with squeezy pouches of saline and blood for transfusions. Dad was a blood donor— Jarli wondered if he might get some of his own blood back.

"Sit down and put on your seat belt," Susan told him, pointing to a chair that folded out of the wall.

Jarli did. Tyson started the engine and zoomed out toward the highway.

"You'll be examined when we get to the hospital," Susan said. "I have to look after your dad right now. But if you start to feel faint or dizzy, let me know ASAP. Got it?"

"Got it."

Susan turned to Dad and started quizzing him. She asked when his birthday was, where he lived, the name of the prime minister, and today's date. Dad got all the questions right, but he always hesitated. Sometimes Susan had to ask him twice. And he spoke clumsily, like maybe he'd bitten his tongue or broken a tooth.

While Susan was interrogating Dad, Jarli called Mum. Her phone rang and rang. She wasn't good at keeping it with her. He had never wanted to hear her voice so badly.

"Come on, Mum," he muttered. "Pick up."

"This is not Josie Wilburn," his mother's voice said cheerily. "This is Josie Wilburn's answering machine. The real Josie can't pick up, but if you leave a brief message—"

Jarli ended the call. He tried his sister's number instead. She picked up immediately. "Hey, bro. 'Sup?"

"Kirstie," Jarli said. "I just tried to call Mum. There's been—"

"Oh, hang on, I'll get her. Mum! *Muuuuuuuum!*"

Mum came on the line. "Jarli! How'd the parent-teacher night go? Be warned—I will check with your father."

Jarli could tell from her voice that she was half kidding—but only half.

"It, um . . ." Jarli began. The parent-teacher night already felt like years ago. "It was fine, I guess. I don't know. It doesn't matter. There's been—"

"It most certainly does matter, young man. If you keep antagonizing Mr. Kendrick in history class, he's not going to give you good grades. And if you really want to study coding at a decent university, you need to keep that grade average up. I know it seems like a long way off, but—"

"Mum," Jarli said. "There's been an accident."

"What kind of accident?"

"A car accident." His phone beeped: *Lie*. He had programmed the app to monitor phone calls. "I mean, not an accident. Someone rammed our car. Dad is hurt."

There was a long, scary silence.

"Mum?" Jarli said. "Are you still there?"

"I'm here," Mum said quietly. "Where are you?"

"I'm in the ambulance. We're on our way to the hospital. Dad's talking, but he seems confused."

"What about you?"

"I'm fine. Can you meet us at the hospital?"

"I'm on my way. What do the paramedics say?" Her voice was shaky.

Jarli didn't want to lie to her, but the truth was hard to say. "They told me he'll be fine," he said eventually. "But come quick, okay?"

"We're on our way. Kirstie! Get in the car. See you soon, Jarli."

As soon as Jarli hung up, his phone chimed. A text message must have come through while he was talking to Mum—

Wrong. *Ninety* messages had come through.

Jarli stared at the screen. Could word about the car crash have spread so fast? He didn't think he even knew ninety people.

He opened the most recent message. It was from Bess, who had been his best friend since they were toddlers.

> Dude, answer your phone!

Jarli scrolled back through the other messages from her.

> A lady from the news came to school looking for you. Something about your app?

> Hey, you're famous! Your app has 900 downloads and counting! No wonder she wants to talk to you.

> Are you seeing this? 11,000 downloads!

> Hey, now that you're a celebrity, can you mention my blog? I'd love some readers.

> Fine. It was just a thought. Whatever.

> 800,000 DOWNLOADS. Dude! Where are you?

> Oh, I get it. Now that you're famous, you're too busy to talk to me.

> I know you're getting my messages. You're always on your phone. It's like it's replaced your brain.

Bess often played pranks on Jarli. This might be one of

them. But if so, she'd gotten a lot of other people involved. There were messages from dozens of senders. Jarli was about to open one when the phone started ringing in his hand.

The screen said *private number*, which probably meant Bess was calling him from her landline to save her cell phone bill. Bess's mum ran a taxi service, so calls always came from a private number.

He answered. "Hello?"

"Mr. Durras!" a voice said. "I'm so pleased I managed to get through to you."

"Uh, hi," Jarli said. "Who's this?"

"This is Dana Reynolds from *Nationwide*. Thank you for taking the time to speak with us today."

Jarli looked at his father, strapped to the stretcher. "Actually," he said, "I'm, uh, kind of in the middle of something."

"It'll only take a minute," Reynolds said cheerily.

Jarli's app beeped. *Lie.*

"Uh, gotta go," Jarli said, and hung up.

He opened a web browser and put his own name into the search field. In the five seconds it took him to type it in and hit search, three more messages came through. Two were from journalists and one was from his school principal.

> Jarli, it's Mrs. Genetti. We'd like to profile you in the newsletter—your project could be good publicity for the school!

Jarli knew that Kelton High School needed some good press. A national newspaper had recently referred to it as having "a culture of bullying" after a kid had been pushed down the stairs. But Jarli's app wasn't a school project. And he didn't want to make himself a target for bullies by looking like a teacher's pet in the school newsletter.

Ignoring the principal's message, Jarli scrolled down to the search results. Because of his unusual first name, the search engine would usually say, "Including results for Charlie Durras," who was some middle-aged guy working for an IT company in the Bahamas. Jarli himself would be way, way down the list. There would eventually be a mention of his podcast, which had only eight subscribers.

But today there were hundreds of results, all for Jarli's own name. Some were even in other languages.

Search *Jarli Durras*

New app exposes lies

This amazing app will tell you when someone is lying

Teenager invents miracle app

5 free apps that will improve your relationship

Jarli leaned against the wall of the ambulance, stunned. This wasn't a prank. His lie detector app had gone viral. But how? And why now? It had been two weeks since he uploaded the source code to an obscure forum.

He tapped on one of the search results and scanned the article. Apparently someone from a tech news site had noticed his app last night and published a post about it this afternoon. A bunch of other news sites had copied the article. Now the app had—

Two million downloads? Jarli did a double-take. But the figures were right.

If this had happened yesterday, he would have been thrilled. But today he was in the back of an ambulance with Dad, who might be bleeding into his brain. He didn't have time for this.

He typed a quick message back to Bess.

Going to hospital. Car crash. Dad's hurt. I'm okay.

The phone started ringing again. *Private number.* Maybe Dana Reynolds again. Jarli rejected the call and put the phone back on airplane mode.

The ambulance swerved, zooming up one of the hospital's driveways. Kelton Research Hospital was a sprawling, two-story building on top of a hill. It had been here since the old days, when Kelton was a coal-mining town. Apparently that was why the hospital was so big—injuries had been common down in the mines. There was a helicopter landing pad on top and a dirt parking lot out front. Nothing else around but bushland.

When the ambulance got to the front of the hospital, the two paramedics jumped out, opened the rear doors, and slid Dad's stretcher out of the back. Jarli followed as they wheeled it inside.

"It's going to be okay, Jarli," Dad said. His voice was muffled. At some point the paramedics had put a transparent plastic mask over his mouth.

Jarli's app didn't work in airplane mode, so he couldn't be sure if Dad was lying. But he probably was—Mum and Dad always made a big deal out of small things, and a small deal about big things. Whenever they said there was nothing to worry about, Jarli knew it was time to panic.

He squeezed Dad's hand. "Mum's coming," he said. "Kirstie, too. They'll be here really soon."

Reception was a wide room with soothing blue walls and a strong smell of disinfectant. The rows of padded plastic chairs were all empty. There wasn't even a receptionist.

Two people in turquoise hospital scrubs ran up to the gurney, stethoscopes swinging around their necks. "Is this the car crash?" one asked.

"Yep," Susan said. "This is Glen Durras, that's his son, Charlie Durras—he was the other occupant of the car."

Before Jarli had a chance to correct her about his name, one of the newcomers rounded on him. "Charlie, take a seat," she said. "I'm Dr. Reid. I'm just going to ask you some questions, okay?"

"Uh, okay," Jarli said.

Reid had sunken eyes, close-cropped hair, and a clipboard. She sat down and gestured to the chair next to her.

The two paramedics were pushing Dad's stretcher away through a pair of double doors. Jarli got a quick glimpse of a corridor with more doors and other corridors leading off it. "Where are they taking him?" Jarli asked.

"To intensive care."

"I want to go with him."

"You can see him soon," Reid said. "Don't worry, he's in good hands."

Dad's stretcher disappeared and the doors slammed shut. Jarli heard an automatic lock click. He reluctantly sat next to Reid.

"Were you in the front seat next to your dad?" she asked.

"Yeah."

"Tell me everything you remember," Reid said.

While Jarli explained, she got him to turn his head left and right, then tilt it forward and back. She squeezed his fingers one by one, then held his wrists and moved them, apparently checking that the joints in his arms still worked. She didn't react when Jarli told her about the old man who had tried to kill them. Maybe she had only asked him to tell her about the crash so he would be distracted.

"Your legs, now," she said. "Tell me if anything hurts."

She lifted his left ankle, then his right. His joints worked normally.

"You've been very lucky," she said.

Jarli stared at her. "Someone tried to kill me."

"Maybe—but there have been two other car accidents near the motel this year. Both fatal."

"Has someone called the police? I need to tell them what happened."

"I'll check." Reid handed him her clipboard. "Fill this in while you wait."

She disappeared through the double doors where the paramedics had taken Dad. The lock *clunked* behind her.

The admission forms had more than fifty questions. Some of them Jarli had no idea how to answer. Did his parents have private health insurance? Who was Dad's regular doctor? He wasn't even sure what to write next to NAME. Was that for Jarli's name or Dad's?

NEXT OF KIN. The words stank of death. Jarli was finding it hard to breathe. Where was Mum?

Overwhelmed, he got up and staggered outside. He took a few deep breaths. His eyes were burning. He didn't want to be crying when Mum and Kirstie turned up—they would assume Dad was dead.

A cool breeze washed up the hill toward the hospital, chilling the tears on his cheeks. He wiped them away and turned to face the parking lot, looking for Mum's car.

It wasn't there.

But there was a brown truck with a huge chrome bull bar.

Followed

The fear hit Jarli like a punch. He almost fell over backward. It was as though he'd seen a ghost—a really scary one, like the headless horseman or the little girl who crawls out of the TV.

The old man had followed them here. Why?

It was definitely the same truck, parked in the shadows away from the hospital lights. The bull bar was slightly dented, and flecked with white paint from Dad's car. The engine was ticking quietly as it cooled. The cab was empty.

Jarli looked around. The lot was quiet and still. Moths buzzed around the dim lights. There were a few other cars, but no people. The old man with the black glasses was nowhere to be seen.

Maybe he was in the hospital, looking for Dad.

Heart racing, Jarli bolted back inside. The reception area was still empty. He ran over to the double doors that all the adults had disappeared through. He jiggled the handle. Locked.

A small window was built into one of the doors. Jarli

rapped loudly on the glass. "Hey!" he yelled. "Let me in!"

He couldn't see anybody, and there was no sign that anyone had heard him.

The lock on the double doors was electronic, but that didn't mean Jarli could hack it. There were no buttons—just a sensor for a swipe card. His coding skills were useless here.

Instead, he ran over to the reception desk and rang the little silver bell. *Ding!* The sound echoed away into nothing.

"Come on," Jarli muttered. He rang the bell again. His ribs still ached from the seat belt. He rubbed the bruised flesh through his shirt.

A TV behind the counter showed grainy security footage from around the hospital. He could see an orderly pushing an empty stretcher down a corridor, then the feed cut to two doctors exiting an elevator. Soon it switched back to show the reception desk, leaving Jarli looking at his own anxious face.

No help was coming. He needed to call the police. Jarli dug out his phone, unlocked it, and brought up the call screen. He was about to punch in 911 when he remembered that his phone was in airplane mode. As he navigated to the settings menu and turned it off, he realized he could probably call emergency services even in airplane mode. In fact, the phone didn't even need to be unlocked. He was panicking. Making mistakes.

Jarli hit nine and one—then movement caught his eye on the TV screen. He looked up from the phone. He couldn't help it. It was just a reflex.

The TV screen was showing the reception area again. Jarli could see himself, part of the counter, and the rows of empty chairs behind him.

But there was something else on the screen. A man, standing behind Jarli.

The picture was blurry, but Jarli recognized him. It was the old man with the black glasses.

As Fast As You Can

Maybe Jarli should have pretended he hadn't seen the man. He could have let the guy think he was sneaking up on him, and then whirled around and stunned the man with a judo chop.

But Jarli wasn't Batman. He wasn't even Robin. He was just a kid who liked making apps.

So as soon as he saw the man on the TV, he turned around—losing the element of surprise.

The old man carried a bottle of bleach in one hand and a cloth in the other. He looked like a cleaner, except that his gloves were leather rather than latex and Jarli could see the collar of a business shirt peeking out from under his overalls. The man was tall with a slight stoop that might have come from a lifetime of ducking under things. A squint shrunk his eyes to the size of raisins.

He looked Jarli up and down, then nodded slightly.

"Jarli Durras?" he said.

Jarli had never been less pleased to have his name pro-

nounced right. "No, sorry," he said, trying not to look terrified. "I'm . . . Henry."

It was just the first name that popped into his head. His
phone beeped in his pocket. *Lie.*

"Oh, okay," the man said, not believing him. Maybe he
had heard the beep and knew what it meant. "Come with me,
Henry."

"I'm waiting for someone," Jarli said.

"It'll only take a minute." The old man's voice was rough
and gurgly, like his lungs were full of water.

"All right," Jarli said shakily. "Sure."

Then he ran the other way, toward the front door.

The man might have been old, but his reflexes were quick.
Jarli heard him give chase a split second later, his rubber-soled
boots slapping the linoleum. Jarli was a strong runner—it was
the only sport he was good at, since it didn't involve throwing
or catching a ball—but the automatic door was closed, trap-
ping him in the reception area. He had to wait for the door to
slide open while the old man's long legs brought him closer
and closer.

As soon as the gap was wide enough, Jarli slipped through
and sprinted out toward the parking lot. "Help!" he yelled.
"Somebody help me!"

He looked around, desperate. No one was there. He
couldn't run back down the driveway—the old man could

drive after him and run him over. And Dad was still inside, vulnerable. Instead Jarli turned left and sprinted up a grassy slope alongside the outer wall of the hospital.

He had hoped the old man would find it hard to run uphill, but it was tough for Jarli, too. His heartbeat was deafening in his ears. It felt like someone was winding chains around his chest, tighter and tighter.

"I'm not going to hurt you!" the man yelled.

Jarli's phone beeped in his pocket. *Lie.* This was a nightmare.

He reached the corner of the building and turned left again, out of sight. A cluster of trees stood forty or fifty yards away. They looked dense enough to hide in. But what if the old man heard him? What if he had a flashlight? Jarli was wearing pale gray jeans and an orange sweater—he would stand out, even in the darkness.

There was a back door to the hospital up ahead, but it might be locked. If it was, he would be trapped out in the open, with no time to get to the trees. The old man would see him.

Jarli had to choose. Run for the trees, or try the door?

Door. He pumped his legs as fast as he could. He could feel the old man getting closer. If Jarli could get inside before the bad guy rounded the corner, he might think Jarli had gone into the trees instead.

There was a sign above the door. From this angle, Jarli

couldn't read it. Hopefully it said, THIS DOOR IS KEPT UNLOCKED BUT CAN BE LOCKED FROM THE INSIDE IF A PSYCHOPATH IS CHASING YOU.

Heart pounding, lungs wheezing, Jarli finally reached the door. There was a pane of glass at face-height, but the lights inside were dead. He couldn't see what lay beyond.

"Please, please, please," Jarli whispered. He twisted the handle and pushed.

The door wouldn't open.

"No!" Jarli cried. He pulled instead.

The door clicked and swung back, hinges squeaking.

Blam! Jarli screamed as the window of the open door shattered next to his head. Shards of glass flew in all directions. A sliver barely missed his eye and left a long scratch on his brow. The bang echoed across the grassy plain, and it took Jarli a second to realize the old man was shooting at him.

Jarli darted through the doorway. He pulled the door closed behind him, but couldn't see a lock. He looked around for something to throw in front of the door to jam it closed. There was a filing cabinet, a fridge, and a desk—but then he remembered that the door opened outward. None of those would help.

He kept running. Motion-activated lights flickered to life around him. He was in some kind of locker room with square, stainless steel doors lining the walls. Maybe the hospital staff kept their clothes here. The air was freezing and smelled of chlorine, like a swimming pool. The tiles were slick and shiny underfoot.

Jarli turned a corner, desperate to get out of sight. He ran through a short corridor into another room—

And suddenly realized where he was.

In the center of the room was a steel slab, lit by a blinding spotlight. Scales hung from the ceiling. Knives and saws hung from hooks on the walls, alongside more steel doors.

Jarli was in the hospital morgue, where they put people after they'd died. Those knives were for cutting up dead bodies. Horrified, Jarli backed away, and yelped as he bumped into something—a hanging tray for weighing organs. It swung from side to side, chains rattling.

There was an elevator on the far side of the room. Jarli didn't see any other way out of there. He ran over and pushed the button. Somewhere above, he heard a clank and a hum as the elevator came to life.

It sounded slow. Would it arrive before the old man did?

The hinges of the outer door squeaked. More broken glass tinkled to the floor. The old man was coming.

Jarli pushed the button rapidly. *Clackclackclack.* But the elevator didn't come any faster. If he didn't find somewhere to hide now, the old man would get him before you could say *Gee, a morgue would be an ironic place to die.* He looked around and saw . . .

One of the square steel doors was slightly ajar.

Jarli hesitated. A morgue drawer seemed like a good hiding place. It would take the old man a long time to search all of them, and he might even assume that Jarli had escaped in the elevator.

But what if the drawer was . . . occupied?

There was no time to come up with another plan. Jarli ran over and wrenched the door the rest of the way open. The steel was so cold that his sweaty fingers left imprints on the handle.

There was no mysterious shape covered by a white sheet. No cold, gray foot with a tag around the toe. The morgue drawer was empty.

Jarli exhaled in momentary relief and climbed in, feetfirst. The space was horribly cramped and dark. Ignoring the tight feeling in his chest, he pulled the door shut, sealing himself into the blackness.

An automatic lock clicked. HE WAS TRAPPED!

It took all his willpower not to start pounding on the inside of the door. He hadn't known it would lock. There wasn't much air in here. It was designed for people who didn't need to breathe. The ceiling was so close to his nose that it felt like being buried alive. Maybe facing the old man would be better than suffocating in this gloomy prison.

Jarli held his breath. He tried to listen for the old man, but it was hard to hear anything over his own panicked heartbeat. *Ka-thump. Ka-thump. Ka-thump.*

Ding! The elevator arrived. Jarli heard the groaning and shuddering as the doors opened.

Footsteps echoed through the morgue. They got closer and closer to where Jarli hid, and then stopped.

Jarli lay perfectly still. The elevator was still here, so the old man would know he hadn't taken it. But would he work out where Jarli had actually gone?

Jarli remembered the handprint he'd left on the icy handle of the door to the drawer. Hopefully it had faded by now. Otherwise it would be obvious where he was hiding.

There was a long, scary silence.

Jarli started to wonder if the old man had left. That would be good—except that Jarli was still locked in the morgue drawer.

He could always call for help, right? Very slowly, Jarli pulled out his phone. The glow of the screen reflected off the steel walls around him. No reception.

He locked the phone again, and it made a cheerful *click.* Jarli's heart leaped into his mouth.

Footsteps approached. The old man had heard the sound.

Jarli squeezed his eyes shut, as though that would make him invisible. It was like being a rabbit, hiding in a burrow while a fox sniffed around nearby. He felt like he was going to have a heart attack.

There was another agonizing silence.

Then a handle clanked. A nearby drawer slid open, wheels

scraping on runners. After a moment, Jarli heard it roll back into place.

Another clank, another scrape. Another drawer had opened, closer this time. The old man was checking the drawers, one by one.

Jarli whimpered. He couldn't help it.

Clank. Scrape.

Jarli got out his phone again. If he called the police right now, the call wouldn't go through. But the phone would keep trying until the reception came back. Maybe the old man wouldn't kill him right away. Maybe the police could trace the location of the phone. As an app developer, Jarli knew that they could use his phone's GPS, Wi-Fi, and signal towers to pinpoint his location within three meters.

Jarli hit the emergency call button just as the door opened next to his head, flooding the drawer with light.

Under Suspicion

Jarli screamed.

So did the old man—because it wasn't the old man. It was a doctor, his gray eyes wide with shock. He hadn't expected to find a live person in one of his morgue drawers.

"Hey!" he yelled, recovering. "What are you doing in there? Get out, this instant!"

Jarli popped his head out of the drawer and looked around. The old man was gone. He must have fled when the doctor arrived in the elevator.

"Out!" the doctor snapped. "Right now!"

He was a balding man with an earring, a cotton mask, and a white smock. His name tag said: LADD.

Jarli scrambled out of the morgue drawer. He was so relieved he could hardly stand up. "Someone tried to kill me," he said. "He's still in the hospital. You have to call the police!"

"The police are already here," Dr. Ladd said angrily. "Probably looking for *you*. This way. Now."

He glared at Jarli and pointed at the elevator with a latex-gloved finger. He seemed unnecessarily angry. Maybe his unpleasant manner was why the hospital made him deal with dead patients rather than live ones.

Ladd herded Jarli into the elevator, stepped in after him, and pushed a button. The doors slid closed and the elevator hummed upward.

"Did you see the old man?" Jarli asked. "With the glasses and the overalls?"

"I saw *you* hiding in my autopsy room," Ladd said. "Since you're not dead, you're in big trouble."

"Was there a cleaner?" Jarli pressed. "When you got out of the elevator?"

Ladd snorted. "Blame the cleaner, huh? That's original."

The elevator stopped, and the doors opened. Ladd prodded Jarli out, pushing harder than necessary, and marched him up the corridor.

Jarli looked around. No sign of the old man. The hospital was as quiet as a tomb. Most of the lights were turned down so patients could sleep. It was now late at night—or maybe Jarli was just exhausted.

Ladd pulled Jarli around a corner into a ward and pulled back a curtain, revealing a hospital bed under a dark window. Two police officers sat in plastic chairs, both fiddling with their phones.

"Officers," Ladd announced. "I found this boy hiding in my morgue. One of the windows was broken. I trust charges will be laid?"

The two cops glanced at Jarli. But Jarli ignored them. He was looking at the hospital bed. A heart monitor was attached to the patient's finger, beeping quietly. The man's eyes were closed. A narrow tube led from an IV bag to the crook of his elbow. A breathing pipe had been attached to the transparent mask on his face.

"Dad," Jarli whispered.

"He's in an induced coma," said a voice from behind Jarli.

He turned around and saw a beak-nosed man wearing navy hospital scrubs. His name badge read: NURSE AMON.

"You're Glen's son?" Amon said.

Jarli nodded. "Jarli."

"Hi, Charlie," Amon said, mishearing him. "The doctors were worried that your dad might be bleeding inside his skull, so they put him in a deep sleep to reduce the pressure. He's just had a scan that showed no bleeding. So now we're bringing him out of the coma, but we have to do it slowly. You understand?"

Jarli nodded. He didn't trust himself to speak.

Ladd was tapping his foot, still waiting for the police to arrest Jarli. "Well?" he said finally.

"We'll take it from here," one of the cops said dryly.

Ladd nodded, straightened his lab coat, and swept out.

Nurse Amon squeezed his shoulder. "I'll be close by, okay, Charlie?" he said.

"Okay."

Amon went away and Jarli turned back to Dad. He kept his eyes on Dad's chest, which was rising and falling gently under the thin hospital gown. Jarli didn't want to look away in case the movement stopped.

He couldn't remember exactly what he'd last said to his father. It was something about Mr. Kendrick's e-mails. Jarli had been angry, and he'd made a sarcastic remark. What if he never got a chance to say sorry?

After a minute, one of the officers cleared her throat.

"Mr. Durras," she said to Jarli. "I'm Constable Blanco, this is Constable Frink. We have some questions for you."

It took Jarli fifteen minutes to explain everything that had happened. The two police officers didn't interrupt. They just sat and watched, as still and emotionless as the statues in Mum's garden.

Their stares made Jarli feel guilty, even though he hadn't done anything wrong. A couple of times his phone beeped in his pocket. He was telling the truth, but the app could sense how nervous he was, and it assumed he was lying.

Jarli took the phone out of his pocket and put it on the table so the front-facing camera could see him. The app was more accurate when the phone could track the face of the person talking.

"Turn that off, please," Constable Frink said. He was a bulky, blond-haired man with a scar on the back of one hand and a faded rose tattoo inside his wrist. He was scratching his chin as though wondering how long it had been since he shaved.

Jarli hesitated. "It has my lie detector app on it. It proves I'm telling the truth."

Frink didn't look impressed. "It's your own app, on your own device. It proves nothing. Put it away, please."

Jarli turned the sound off and slid the phone back into his pocket.

"So," Constable Blanco said. As she opened her mouth, Jarli could see that she had a chipped front tooth. She was sitting perfectly upright in her chair, like a straight-A student. Her eyes were dark and watchful.

"You think this man drove into your car deliberately?" she said.

Jarli's jaw fell open. Had she not been listening?

"He crashed into us *twice*," Jarli said. "He would have done it three times if Anya hadn't showed up. You have to search the hospital for him!"

"The building is surrounded. If he's still here, he's not going anywhere."

Jarli didn't think there were enough cops in Kelton to surround the whole hospital. She must mean that the front and back doors were guarded. But what if the old man rappelled down the side of the building or something?

"So the man works here?" Frink asked. "As a cleaner?"

"He was *disguised* as a cleaner," Jarli said. "He was wearing normal clothes under his overalls. I said that already."

"How could you tell?"

"His collar was poking out. Can't you watch the video? From the security cameras?"

"The camera in reception shows you running away," Frink said, "and a man following you out. But it's a low-resolution camera. He could be anybody."

"What about in the morgue?"

"No cameras there."

Blanco adjusted her police cap, which was so clean that it looked brand new. "How did you know it was the same man who caused the crash?"

"I saw his car in the parking lot," Jarli said.

"The truck with the bull bar, right?"

"Right."

"There are a lot of trucks like that in Kelton. And plenty of people in the hospital. Even if it was the same truck from the accident—"

"It wasn't an accident."

"The truck could have belonged to anyone. How did you know it was this guy in particular?"

"I recognized his glasses. Then he chased me."

"Uh-huh. So you went around the back, broke in through a window—"

"No, I opened the door," Jarli said. "He broke the window. He was shooting at me."

"What kind of gun did he have?"

"I didn't see."

Blanco glanced at her partner again. "No one else has reported hearing a gunshot."

"Have you asked around?"

"Everyone's asleep."

"Well," Jarli said, "that would explain why they didn't hear it."

"Jarli!"

Jarli turned around. His mother and his sister hurried through the ward toward him, escorted by Amon.

His mother wore a red dress that reached her sandals. She usually washed off her makeup after finishing her shift at the post office, but today she hadn't. Tears had left dark streaks on her cheeks.

Kirstie looked like she'd just walked out of a horror movie. Her eyes were wide and her mouth hung open. She moved as though she'd forgotten how her legs worked. She wore an oversize T-shirt with the lead singer from Paint Rocket on it, clashing with her bright blue school trousers—Mum must have grabbed her when she was only halfway through getting changed.

Mum hugged Jarli. Kirstie stared numbly at Dad.

"You're okay," Mum whispered, kissing the top of Jarli's head. "You're okay."

"Mum," Jarli said, embarrassed. "The police are here."

Mum noticed the police for the first time. "Who are you? What do you want?"

"We're investigating the accident," Constable Blanco said.

"It wasn't an accident," Jarli said for what felt like the billionth time. "Mum, a man tried to kill me and Dad. He rammed our car deliberately, and then he followed us here. He tried to shoot me."

Mum's eyes widened. "Is that why there's such a big crowd outside?" she asked the police.

Blanco avoided the question. "We're still trying to find other witnesses to corroborate your son's story, Mrs. Durras."

Jarli didn't like the way she said "story." It was as though she thought he'd made the whole thing up.

"It's Mrs. Wilburn," Mum said. She had kept her name when she married Dad. Only telemarketers called her "Mrs. Durras."

"My husband will tell you what happened," she continued. "Why is he still unconscious? Jarli said he was talking."

Dad groaned. It was as though Mum's voice had brought him back to life.

"Glen!" Mum cried. She squeezed his hand tightly. Jarli and Kirstie crowded around the other side of the bed, forgetting the cops.

Dad smiled. "Hey, Josie," he croaked. "Hey, kids. What's going on?"

"You're in the hospital," Kirstie said.

"There was a car crash," Mum said. "Don't you remember?"

"A car crash?" Dad squinted up at Mum. "Is everyone okay?"

Mum sighed. "Looks like it." She went to squeeze Dad's arm and then realized the needle was in the way. She patted him on the head instead.

"Mr. Durras," Blanco said. "I'm Constable Blanco. Do you remember anything about the other driver?"

Dad hesitated. "What driver?"

"The driver of the other vehicle. In the crash."

"Sorry," Dad said. "I don't remember the crash."

Jarli's heart sank. If Dad didn't remember, Jarli was the only one who knew what the old man looked like.

Then Jarli's phone vibrated in his pocket.

Jarli gasped. *Dad was lying. But why?*

"Excuse us, Mr. Durras," Blanco said.

The two police officers stood up and made their way out of the ward. Jarli heard a door closing.

"I'm just going to the bathroom," he announced. He hurried to the far end of the ward. When he was out of Mum and Kirstie's sight, he pressed his ear against the closed door.

The cops were talking in the corridor, but Jarli couldn't tell what they were saying. He dug out his phone, opened *Truth* and held the phone against the door to the ward.

Words started appearing on the screen.

>You think he's lying?
>The dad, or the kid?
>Either one.

This was a bug rather than a feature. Jarli had discovered it after leaving his phone on the kitchen bench next to an old radio. *Truth* had transcribed every word of the broadcast, even though the radio's volume control was turned almost all the way down. The phone's microphone had picked up the vibrations through the bench.

>You saw the crash site. No sign of another vehicle.
>Other than the damage to the car. Looked like multiple collisions to me.
>Yeah, but we don't know they were all from tonight. The major impact was probably from the streetlight outside the motel. The minor damage could be from years of careless driving.
>Why would the kid lie?
>I'm not saying he's lying. He could be in shock.
>The dad might know more than he's saying. Let's get his family away from him. See if that loosens his tongue.
>Okay. But we shouldn't spend too much time on this case. It's probably just an accident. Hugo Niehls's disappearance is more important.

Hugo Niehls. It took Jarli a moment to place the name.

Dad had mentioned it in one of his late-night phone calls. Dad worked for a data-security company, so it wasn't unusual for him to be secretive. But now one of the people he *had* talked about was missing. Was that a coincidence?

>You happy with that?
>Yeah. Let's get rid of the family.

Jarli quickly stepped away from the door and ran back through the ward toward the hospital bed.

"Where have you been?" Kirstie pointed. "The bathroom is that way."

"Oh," Jarli said. "Hey, what's that out the window?"

He was trying to distract her, but there really was something out there. A strange light, blinking between the blinds.

Kirstie, Mum, and Dad all looked.

"Plane," Mum said.

"UFO," Kirstie said at the same time.

Jarli opened the blinds. Dozens of people stood on the lawn below. Some held video cameras or microphones. Others lifted smartphones up high for a better view. The light was from a drone, filming the hospital from above.

As soon as the people saw Jarli, they started yelling. All those wide eyes and open mouths alarmed him—it was like something out of a zombie game. He backed away from the window.

When the police had told Jarli the hospital was surrounded, this was what they meant.

Blanco was standing behind him. "More reporters. That's all we need." She walked over to the window and opened it wide. "Hey!" she yelled. "Get lost! You can't show the faces of anyone who hasn't been charged yet. You know that. We'll make a statement when there's something worth saying."

She slammed the window closed and shut the blinds. One word stayed stuck in Jarli's mind: *hasn't been charged* yet.

Mum was astonished. "I didn't know there were that many reporters in Kelton," she said.

"There aren't," Blanco replied. "They've come from all over the state."

"To cover a car crash?"

Jarli sank down into his chair, wanting to disappear. They weren't here for the car crash.

Kirstie had already found the remote for the TV on the wall opposite Dad's bed. She turned it on and clicked through the channels until she found the news.

"Check it out," she said. "We're on TV!"

". . . only minutes after we spoke to him on the phone," said a woman with perfectly coiffed hair and bright red lipstick. "At this stage, Jarli's condition is still unknown."

In the background, Jarli could see the outside of Kelton hospital. It was surrounded by hundreds of people.

Jarli recognized the woman's voice. She was Dana Reynolds,

the reporter who had called him in the ambulance.

The headline down the bottom of the screen said: *Truth-App Boy Fights for His Life After Car Accident*.

"We'll have more on this story after the break," Reynolds said grimly. The TV cut to an ad for dishwashing detergent.

Jarli felt sick. It was as though the TV had convinced him that he really was dying.

Mum sat down next to Dad's legs. She looked at Jarli.

"Well, Truth-app boy," she said. "What have you done this time?"

Beneath the Radar

Did you ever stop to think about what you were doing?" Mum demanded.

They were back in reception, waiting for the police to finish questioning Dad in the ward. Jarli hoped he would tell them something about the old man, but he still seemed pretty out of it.

"What do you mean?" Jarli asked.

"When you were making that app. Did you, at any point, wonder if it was a good idea?"

This sounded like one of Mum's trick questions, where both options were the wrong answer.

"This isn't my fault," Jarli said.

Mum pointed through the glass doors. The parking lot was so full that some of the reporters had parked on the grass. Jarli couldn't see any of them from here, but he could hear the babble of distant voices.

"*That's* your fault," Mum said. "Those people are going crazy over you."

Jarli was annoyed. His app was so great that it had made

him world-famous overnight. Mum was supposed to be proud of him.

"I didn't invite them here," Jarli said. "I only posted the code online so people could help me test it."

"Without thinking about what might happen. Just like when you hacked into Mr. Kendrick's e-mails."

"I guessed his password," Jarli muttered. "That's not really hacking."

"You worked out which web host the school used, got into Mr. Kendrick's mail servers, and deleted one of his e-mails, all without asking yourself: *Is this a good idea?*"

"The e-mail was from me. I sent it to him by accident."

"But you hacked in deliberately."

"If Mr. Kendrick had seen that e-mail, he would have failed me for sure. You're the one always going on about my grades."

"You must have put hours into this lie detector project. If you put the same amount of effort into your schoolwork instead of this dangerous program—"

Jarli snorted. "Dangerous?"

"Did it not occur to you," Mum said, "that almost everyone has secrets? People might not take kindly to an app exposing them."

"Well then, it serves them right for lying in the first place," Jarli said.

"He doesn't get it, Mum," Kirstie said, yawning. "He's always been too honest."

"How can you be *too* honest?" Jarli asked.

"Well, if I asked you how my hair looks—"

"Greasy," Jarli said immediately. Kirstie clearly hadn't washed her long black hair in a few days.

Mum stifled a snort.

"See?" Kirstie said. "Now I'm mad at you. But if you'd lied, I would have been happy. And you wouldn't be about to get punched."

She hit Jarli in the upper arm. Jarli yelped. His shoulder was still sore from the crash.

"Kirstie, don't hit your brother," Mum said automatically. Jarli had heard her mutter those words in her sleep once.

"But if people are allowed to lie," Jarli said, "then no one will ever tell you how bad your hair looks, and you'll never get around to washing it."

"Of course I will," Kirstie said. "I'm not a slob."

"And when I tell you that your hair looks good," Jarli said, "you can trust me. Because you know I'm willing to tell you when it looks bad."

"When have you ever told me my hair looks good?"

"It's a hypothetical. I mean . . ." Jarli trailed off. Something Mum said had finally caught up with him. *Almost everyone has secrets.*

What if that was the reason for the attack? What if the old man had a secret, something Jarli's app had exposed?

If he wanted revenge, he would keep coming. He had a

truck, a gun, and who knew what other weapons. And since no one else believed he existed, it wouldn't be long before he caught up with Jarli again.

Before Jarli could finish this thought, the two police officers emerged from Dad's ward.

"You can go back in now," Constable Blanco said. She gave Mum a card. "Call us if your husband remembers anything else."

Jarli remembered everything, but she didn't give *him* a card. She left without even asking him to describe the old man in detail. She clearly didn't trust his version of events.

It was so unfair. Jarli had made the app not just because he hated being lied to, but because he hated being disbelieved. The app had made him a celebrity, and now people seemed to trust him less than ever.

He followed Mum and Kirstie back into the darkened ward. Dad was asleep. Mum and Kirstie sat next to him. Kirstie pulled out her phone and started playing a game. Jarli wondered how much longer they would have to stay here. He couldn't shake the feeling that the old man was still around, waiting for another chance to strike. Jarli wouldn't feel safe until he was at home, with all the doors and windows locked.

Mum looked like she wanted to continue their conversation, but didn't want to risk waking Dad. So she just sighed and looked out the window.

Relieved, Jarli brought up a social media app on his phone.

Ignoring the thousands of notifications, he typed in a quick post. The police might not believe Jarli about the old man, but surely someone would.

> I'm fine! Nobody panic. I wasn't hurt in the crash.
> But watch out for the other driver—I think he hit us
> on purpose. He's a tall old man with black-framed
> glasses. He drives a brown truck with a bull bar.

He hit publish, wishing he had thought to check the license plate the second time he saw the truck. After a moment, he wrote a follow-up message:

> It's crazy that so many people downloaded
> TRUTH! I'm glad you all like it. Thanks for your
> support!

Both posts were public. Surely someone would see the old man or his truck around.

Jarli had told Anya he would let her know what happened. He didn't have her number, but he found her profile easily enough. According to social media, they had a couple of mutual friends. Jarli was amused by her profile pic—a photo of a duck—and her motto.

> "Follow your heart, but take your brain with you."

He started typing.

> Hey, Anya. Thanks for your help tonight. You were very calm—are you secretly a superhero or something? (Don't worry, I won't tell anyone.) Anyway, Dad seems fine now. I'm fine too. Thanks again—see you at school.

He figured he should probably message Bess, too.

> Hey, Bess. We're at the hospital now—Dad's fine. Sorry if I freaked you out.

He got a response almost immediately.

> Why would I freak out? Just because my best friend has been rushed to the hospital after a car accident? The TV says you're dying, by the way.

> Not an accident. Some guy tried to kill us. He rammed us with his car, twice!

> :O

> And then followed us to the hospital AND SHOT AT ME.

> You're kidding, right? Tell me you're kidding.

I wish. But the cops don't believe me.

I don't believe you either.

Come on, when have I ever lied to you? But . . .

But?

. . . no one else saw the guy.

This is crazy. What did he look like?

Hang on.

Rummaging through the chest of drawers near Dad's hospital bed, Jarli found a notepad, a bible, and a pen. Dad's phone was in there too, on top of his clothes. Someone had neatly folded them, even though they were ruined. It looked like the doctors had cut them off him with scissors.

Jarli took the pen and started trying to draw the old man's face on the notepad.

It didn't really work. Jarli wasn't a great artist, and the more he tried to picture the guy, the more details slipped away. Were the frames of his glasses round or square? Had the hair poking out from under his baseball cap been gray or brown?

All Jarli remembered clearly was those two tiny eyes, like evil raisins.

He gave up on the drawing and did an image search instead. *Old man black glasses.* He found a picture that looked kind of like the guy, and sent it to Bess.

She responded fast.

> You were attacked by Gary Oldman?

Someone's phone buzzed.

"Turn that off, Jarli," Mum said wearily.

"It's not mine," Jarli said. He opened the drawer and found Dad's phone vibrating on top of his sliced-up clothes. The name on the screen said *Ben Gorman.* Dad's boss at the data security company.

Jarli went to turn the phone off, but Mum saw the name. "Is that Ben?" she said. "It's four a.m. Why is he calling?"

"Maybe he wants to offer me a million dollars for my app," Jarli said pointedly.

"Didn't you already give your app away for free?" Kirstie asked.

Jarli opened his mouth, then closed it again. She was right. He had only shared the code so people could help him test it, but now that it had gone mainstream, he had missed his chance to sell it. His app had gone viral, and he wasn't going to earn anything.

A wave of grief crashed over him. He could have been a millionaire! A billionaire, even. And now . . .

"Answer the phone or give it here," Mum said impatiently.

Jarli answered it. "Hi, Mr. Gorman."

"Jarli, hi." Gorman sounded rattled. "You're all over the news. Is your dad okay?"

"I think so."

"Is he awake? Talking?"

"Not right now."

"What about you? Are you all right? And Josie and Kirstie?"

"I'm fine. Mum and Kirstie weren't in the car."

Jarli heard Gorman breathe out. "That's good. Is your mum there?"

Hearing him, Mum held out her hand for the phone.

"She's here," Jarli said. "But can I ask you a quick question first?"

"Uh, sure," Gorman said.

"Do you think I made a mistake, putting the code for my lie detector app online for free?"

Mum sighed impatiently.

Gorman hesitated for a moment. "Depends what you were trying to achieve," he said finally.

"The news said two million people had downloaded my app," Jarli said. "If I'd been selling it for ninety-nine cents, then I'd have almost two million dollars."

"Or maybe you'd have nothing, because no one buys

anything anymore," Gorman grumbled. "And your app would be full of bugs, because no one had tested it for you. Plus, the people who wrote the speech recognition algorithm you used might be suing you for copying their code. In fact, they might do that anyway."

"I credited the original programmers," Jarli said. His voice came out sounding small.

"Relax, kid," Gorman said. "Did you want to make money, or do you just like writing code?"

"Both, I guess."

"Well, don't worry. You might have opened a can of worms, but at least you got everybody's attention. When you search for coding jobs in the future, this will look really good on your résumé. Put your mum on."

Jarli handed the phone over.

"Ben," Mum said. "Thanks for calling."

There was a pause while Gorman said something Jarli couldn't hear.

"We're trapped in the hospital by an army of reporters," Mum said. "But otherwise, everyone's all right."

She paused and then chuckled. Mum had a throaty laugh that seemed to come right up from her belly, even when it was quiet.

"Yeah, okay," she said. "That'll teach them. See you soon."

PART TWO: PARIAH

I programmed my app to recognize sudden corrections. A correction isn't the same as a lie. For example:

I was at home all day—well, I went to the bakery just before lunch. But other than that I stayed home.

The first six words aren't accurate. But liars don't usually do those sudden corrections unless someone calls them out. So the app will register this story as true.

From the documentation for Truth, *version 1.2*

Escaping Incognito

From the outside, it looked more like a music festival than a hospital. Hundreds of people bustled back and forth, bundled up in polar fleece jackets. Spotlights swept across the crowd. Camera operators struggled to focus on their own reporters, who shouted into hand-held microphones. Print journalists juggled notepads, voice recorders, and vacuum flasks of coffee. But the hospital itself was dark and quiet.

Until it wasn't.

As soon as the steel rollerdoor of the garage started to slide upward, the camera operators swarmed inward. Everyone wanted to be closest. The footage would be most valuable if it didn't include reporters from competing networks.

The ambulance eased forward out of the garage, lights flashing. The siren screamed, but the camera operators wore headphones, and the reporters didn't even seem to notice. They were half-deaf from years of their own bellowed questions.

The ambulance honked its horn as it nudged through the crowd. The reporters weren't stupid. They knew that Kelton was a small town, unlikely to have two medical emergencies in one night. And they knew that Jarli Durras and his family would want to leave the hospital without getting crushed in a media scrum. An ambulance was the perfect escape vehicle.

Tall TV journalists jammed their cameras against the windows, trying to get a shot of Jarli inside. Radio reporters stood farther back, narrating the action into their microphones.

"It looks like Jarli Durras and his family are leaving the hospital in an ambulance," Dana Reynolds was saying gravely, "which could mean that his injuries are even more severe than originally reported. . . ."

A news producer was on her phone. "Durras is leaving now," she said. "He should be back at the house in fifteen minutes. Make sure you get a shot of the ambulance turning into the driveway. He seems like a reluctant subject, so try to hit him with some hard questions when he gets out."

As the reporters started to drift away from the hospital, an electric car emerged from the garage. It was a sleek black sedan with tinted windows.

The driver was Ben Gorman, Dad's boss.

"I think they bought it," Gorman said. "Let's go."

Jarli and his family sat upright in the back seat, peering out of the windows. The reporters were all either running after the ambulance, or hurrying back to their vans to give chase. No one was paying much attention to Gorman's car.

"It was nice of the hospital to provide a decoy ambulance," Mum said.

"They didn't do it for us," Dad said. "They want those reporters gone."

Quietly, Jarli wondered if that was why Dr. Reid had discharged Dad so early. Was it even safe to leave the hospital only hours after coming out of a coma?

"We used this trick all the time when I was in private security." Gorman swerved off the driveway and onto the road toward Jarli's house. "Send an obvious vehicle out first, then put the principal in a normal one."

Jarli wouldn't have described Gorman's car as "normal." The inside had a twelve-speaker sound system, a miniature fridge built into the center console, and laptop holsters in the polished wooden door sills. The engine had started as soon as a hidden camera recognized Gorman's face behind the wheel. It was probably the most expensive car in Kelton. Even with Jarli's whole family in the back, there was plenty of room.

"You used to protect principals?" Jarli said, confused.

Gorman smiled. "That's what my bodyguards used to call their clients."

Gorman had polished white teeth and a short ponytail. Like many modern CEOs he wore jeans and running shoes rather than a suit, but Jarli could tell they were expensive. His shirts fit him so well they must have been tailored, and the shoes were always perfectly white. Maybe Gorman bought a new pair every time he got a grass stain.

Jarli had expected him to send someone else to pick them

up, but maybe no one was available—CipherCrypt employed only half a dozen people. Dad worked largely on his own. Part of his job involved setting up server racks and cooling them with liquid nitrogen. Jarli had never been allowed inside the building, but he'd watched videos on the company website. It had been so strange to see Dad acting all serious and professional: "CipherCrypt is the perfect choice to keep your data safe from hackers."

Dad wouldn't be starring in any more company videos anytime soon. Dr. Reid had said his face might take months to heal completely. And he'd have to wear a cast on his arm for six weeks—Jarli wondered if he could still work. Maybe Gorman had volunteered to drive them so he could get a sense of how useful Dad would be at work.

"Thanks again for coming to get us, Boss," Dad said.

"Don't call me boss," Gorman said cheerfully. "I made some chicken soup for you." There were about fifty cupholders in the car—Gorman pulled a vacuum flask out of one of them and passed it to Dad.

"Thanks, Ben," Mum said.

"I don't know if chicken soup is good for head injuries," Gorman added. "But it's worth a shot, right? I'll pick up the Thermos when we check on you in a couple of days. No need to come into work today, obviously."

"I can work from home," Dad said. He did that two days a week.

"No," Gorman said firmly. He steered the car off the main street toward the suburbs. "You need rest."

Dad squirmed. He seemed uncomfortable that his boss was driving him home, and he still claimed not to remember anything from the car crash. He had refused to verify Jarli's story about the old man.

Dr. Reid had said unreliable memories were a typical side effect of trauma, and she had looked at Jarli as she said this. Mum had noticed, and now even she seemed doubtful that the old man with the black glasses existed. It was infuriating.

"How did you hear about the accident?" Mum said. "You must have been up early."

"Couldn't sleep," Gorman said. "At three a.m. I gave up and turned on the TV. And there was Jarli! Author of the miracle app, fighting for his life after a car accident." He glanced at Jarli in the rearview mirror. "Is your app listening to us right now?"

The phone was sitting next to Jarli on the seat. "No," he said.

The phone beeped. *Lie.*

Jarli grinned. "See how well it works?"

"Impressive," Gorman said. "You should be proud of yourself."

Jarli nudged Mum. Did she get how cool this was yet?

Mum just raised her eyebrows and turned away, watching the houses whip past the window.

"We're not out of the woods yet," Gorman said. "There'll be reporters out the front of your house. Getting through them will be . . . intense. Is there a back way in?"

"We could climb over the neighbor's fence," Kirstie said. "The couple behind our place."

"I can see the headlines now," Mum said dryly. "*Truth app boy caught trespassing on neighbor's property.*"

"I was thinking we'd call them first," Kirstie said. "Obviously."

"Do you know them well?" Gorman asked.

Mum and Dad shook their heads.

"I think they're names are . . . Patrick and Grace?" Dad guessed. "Peter and Grace?"

"My advice?" Mr. Gorman said. "Don't call them. They're likely to sell you out to the reporters. We'll have to go through the front door. Jarli, have you thought about a statement?"

Jarli's eyes widened. "A statement?"

"Journalists are overworked and underpaid. The fastest way to make them go away is to make a statement."

"What should I say?"

"Something like, 'The family requests privacy at this time,'" Dad suggested.

"Nah, that never works," Gorman said. "Give them something they can use, like: 'It's a miracle no one was killed, but I'm just glad everyone is safe. And I'm so excited that people like my app. No further questions.'"

Jarli nodded. "I can do that," he said. But he was terrified. Or was he just hungry? The hollow ache in his guts could have come from fear or hunger. Now that he thought about it, he could kill for a supreme from his local pizza place.

When the car turned onto Jarli's street, the horde of reporters became visible. They were trampling Mum's garden as they shuffled around in tiny, impatient circles. Early-morning dog-walkers had paused to watch the commotion. Dozens of black, shiny camera lenses turned on the car as it approached.

Jarli had always thought being famous would be fun. Celebrities made it look like fun on the Internet. At school, everyone basically ignored Jarli unless he was in trouble. Same deal at home. Mum and Dad were always busy, even when they weren't working. Jarli had fantasized about being admired—envied, even. But after only ten hours of fame he was already dreading the attention.

Mum gave him a hug. Dad squeezed Jarli's hand. "You'll be okay," he said.

The phone didn't beep. Dad was telling the truth—he genuinely thought Jarli could handle what was coming. But this actually made Jarli feel worse. Mum always said that a worry shared is a worry halved. If Dad wasn't scared, then Jarli had to do all the worrying himself.

The driveway was full of people, so Gorman parked on the street instead. Reporters pressed cameras against the windows. The lenses looked like the suckers on a giant tentacle.

It was as though the car was being attacked by a sea monster.

"That's antiflash glass," Gorman said. "They can't see you."

"You ready?" Mum asked.

Jarli took a deep breath, and pushed open the door.

Exposure

The reporters were packed in so tightly that Jarli could barely open the car door. The video cameras had built-in lights that blinded him. As soon as Jarli climbed out of the vehicle, a wall of questions hit him.

"Jarli! Did you know that a prominent tech blogger has labeled your app a hoax?"

"Are you being investigated for violations of the privacy act?"

"How does it feel to be condemned by the President of the United States?"

"Would you say you are a good role model for young people?"

"Did you know this app would endanger your family?"

Reporters stood unpleasantly close to Jarli, holding microphones right up against his face. He couldn't see the ground under his feet, and he was starting to feel like it wasn't there. His knees began to give way, but Dad didn't let him fall. He dragged Jarli through the crowd.

People were yelling at Mum and Kirstie too.

"What's it like having a famous brother?" someone shouted at Kirstie.

"As a wife and mother," someone else roared at Mum, "what effect do you think Jarli's app will have on families? Do you think the divorce rate will go up?"

Mum gritted her teeth, but she was smart enough not to take the bait.

Dad nudged Jarli onto the front porch of their three-bedroom house. The spotlights revealed the peeling paint and the cobwebs at the corners of the windows. They had lived here for Jarli's whole life, and he never thought it looked shabby until now.

"Jarli will make a brief statement," Mum said.

She used her Mum-voice, and it held such authority that the reporters fell silent instantly. The only sound was the clicking of cameras. The front row held up their phones, which had tiny microphones plugged into them. Jarli saw Dana Reynolds in the crowd, her immaculate hair blocking someone else's view.

The lights flicked on in the house next door. The neighbors—Grace and Patrick/Peter, both in their sixties and wearing pajamas—were glaring at Jarli through the window, as though he had invited all these people here.

Jarli stared out at the assembled crowd. What if the old man with the brown truck was here? The street was so packed that he could be hiding anywhere. He could be pointing a gun at Jarli right now.

He's not going to attack me in front of all these people, Jarli told himself.

Dad nudged him, and Jarli remembered that he was supposed to make a statement. But he'd completely forgotten what he was supposed to say.

"Um, hello," he told the crowd. "Thank you for coming."

"Louder!" yelled someone up the back. Other reporters shushed him.

"I never dreamed that so many people would like my app," Jarli began.

His phone beeped in his pocket. *Lie.* He had often fantasized about *Truth* being a huge success.

Several phones beeped in the reporters' hands. They were using the app too.

Jarli could feel his sweat gleaming in the light from the cameras. "I mean, I only wanted a more honest world," he said.

This line sounded good, but it was a mistake. All the phones beeped. *Lie.* Jarli didn't really care about an honest world. He was just sick of people always trying to hide the truth from him, particularly his father.

The reporters were starting to grin.

Jarli had remembered what he was supposed to say now. "Anyway," he said. "It's a miracle no one was hurt. I'm just glad everyone is safe. No further questions."

"Is it true you stole the code for the app?" a reporter yelled.

Jarli wanted to say no. But what if the app contradicted him? On live TV?

"I borrowed the code," he said, knowing how bad that sounded. "But only some of it. And I credited the original programmers. It was open-source."

"People are talking about using your app at the G20 conference next week," another reporter said. "World leaders will check one another's remarks for lies. Do you think your app could start a war?"

"Someone tried to kill me and my dad," Jarli snapped. "Why are you hassling me? Why aren't you talking to the police about *him*?"

"Would you say you've made yourself a target?"

"It's not *my* fault!" Jarli bellowed. "Go away! No more questions."

He turned and tried to run into the house, but no one had unlocked the front door yet. Cameras flashed as he fumbled with his keys. Some reporters were yelling more questions. Others were laughing.

Eventually Jarli got the door open and stumbled into the hallway. His family followed him in and shut the door.

Hooper, Jarli's big black terrier, barked and ran up to Jarli. She wagged her tail as she sniffed his shoes.

"Well," Mum said after a pause. "That wasn't too bad."

Jarli's phone beeped. *Lie.*

Public Enemy

I t was a while before anyone noticed that the TV was missing.

"I don't believe this," Mum groaned. "We've been robbed!"

Jarli stared. There was a clean square among the dust on the cabinet where it used to sit. The game console was gone too, and the sound system.

Dad disappeared into his bedroom. "My work laptop is gone," he called. He sounded scared. Jarli wondered if it could be used to break into CipherCrypt's files.

"They must have seen the news," Mum said. "They knew we were at the hospital and the house was empty."

Jarli felt like she and Kirstie were glaring at him. He escaped into his bedroom.

His computer—the one he'd assembled himself, with the custom graphics card—was gone. Jarli felt sick. He'd poured all his pocket money into that machine. And not all his files were backed up to the cloud. There were programs he'd written and videos he'd made that he would never get back.

"Oh no!" Mum cried from her room. "Where's Nanna's necklace?" Her grief was painful to hear.

Dad was on the phone. "My name is Glen Durras—I need to speak to Constable Blanco."

Jarli rifled through his closet and his desk. He didn't think anything else was missing, but the sense that some stranger had been here was horrible.

Hooper ran into his room, wagging her tail.

"Some guard dog you are," Jarli said.

Hooper woofed. He couldn't resist patting her anyway.

"Come on," he said. "Let's check on Kirstie."

He knocked on Kirstie's door. "Are you missing anything?"

There was no answer. Jarli pushed the door open. Kirstie was sitting on her bed, hugging her legs. To Jarli, her room looked the same as always—Paint Rocket posters on the walls, schoolwork spread across the floor, some dolls she'd outgrown sitting on the shelves next to a model UFO.

"Is anything missing?" Jarli asked.

Kirstie said something so quiet he didn't hear.

"What's gone?"

"My diary," Kirstie whimpered.

Jarli hadn't known she kept a diary. He sat next to his sister and put his arm around her. "I'm sorry, sis," he said.

Kirstie looked like she was trying not to cry. "What if someone puts it online?"

"What was in it?" Jarli asked.

Kirstie didn't answer. She just sat there, trembling.

"I won't let that happen," Jarli said.

"You can't stop it."

"Sure I can. I'll set up an automated alert for anything posted with your name. If your diary shows up, I'll get it deleted or crash the site it's on. Then I'll hack whoever posted it and ruin their lives. I'll mess with their calendar so they go to the dentist every day."

He wasn't sure he could do any of that, but he was desperate to cheer Kirstie up. It didn't work.

"You're not a hacker," she said.

"Tell that to my teachers."

Kirstie lay down in bed and rolled to face the wall. Jarli patted her awkwardly on the shoulder and then left.

He was too freaked out to sleep, so he went to get some breakfast. Cooking usually relaxed him—measuring ingredients, turning up the heat, enjoying the smell of garlic or cinnamon. It was kind of zen. But today it felt mechanical. Even cracking the eggs—usually his favorite part—seemed like a chore.

He scooped the scrambled eggs onto some toast and got out his phone while he ate. Maybe someone had seen the old man or the brown truck.

Scrolling through his notifications he saw hundreds of friend requests from strangers, thousands of new subscribers to his podcast, and heaps of comments posted on his profiles.

Some were encouraging:

OMG, your app is awesomesauce!

Others were sarcastic:

Gee, I wish I was smart enough to get famous by
stealing code and crashing a car.

A few could go either way:

Hey, nice work on TV.

Several people were accusing Jarli of stealing their work
and threatening to sue him. Jarli knew he hadn't done anything wrong—he had written 90 percent of the code himself,
and the rest was open-source—but it was still scary.

Jarli's description of the old man had been shared several
times, but no one seemed to have seen him.

The disastrous televised statement had already been
posted to dozens of sites and viewed by hundreds of thousands of people. Someone had turned the last few seconds
into an animated GIF. Over and over, a terrified-looking Jarli
shouted silently and then tried to flee into his house. The
caption below it read:

not my fault go away no more questions!

Jarli hung his head in his hands. He had become a meme. The whole world was laughing at him.

His appetite was gone. Abandoning the meal, he got out of the chair to wash the pan. Hooper immediately leaped up onto the table and started eating his eggs. As soon as they were finished, she turned to Gorman's chicken soup. Mum had poured it into a bowl, but Dad hadn't eaten it.

"Life's pretty simple for you, huh?" Jarli mumbled.

Hooper didn't even look up from the soup.

Jarli kept his phone by the sink while he washed up. Another post on his profile caught his eye.

What an idiot. Too stupid to live.

Jarli's blood ran cold. Who would say something like that?

There was no way of knowing who had posted the message. There was no profile picture, and the name was clearly made up: *Fool Hardy*. Probably just a troll. But what if it wasn't?

As Jarli watched, another post appeared beside it.

Will someone please kill this moron?

A third person commented on that post.

One of the reporters had location tracking on her

phone when she posted the interview. So I have the kid's home address.

No way. Prove it.

He's on Namadgi Drive in Kelton South.

Jarli leaped out of his chair. These people knew where he lived!

How much does it cost to hire a hit man these days? We could crowdfund it.

"Mum!" he yelled. "Mum!"

Mum hurried out of the bedroom. "Shush!" she said. "Your father's sleeping."

"They're talking about killing me!" Jarli hissed.

"Who is?"

"People on the Internet!"

"Oh, sweetie." Mum rubbed his back. "People can be horrible, but I'm sure they're just joking."

"This isn't a joke, Mum," Jarli said. "They've posted our home address."

Mum looked over his shoulder. Her eyes went wide as she scanned the screen.

"Who are these people?" she demanded.

"I don't know."

The doorbell rang.

They looked at each other.

"Don't answer that," Jarli said.

"Probably just a reporter," Mum said.

It rang again. Mum stood up.

"Don't!" Jarli said.

"I'll just see who it is."

"What if it's the guy who rammed our car? Or one of those psychos from the Internet?"

"The house is surrounded by reporters," Mum said. "They'd have to be crazy to try anything now."

"They *are* crazy!" Jarli insisted.

But Mum was already walking toward the door. She opened the peephole and sighed.

"Just a delivery," she said, and unlocked the door.

"Mum, don't!" Jarli said.

Mum opened the door. Jarli had expected to see the old man disguised as a courier. But the delivery driver was a young woman, holding a plastic parcel about the size of a shoebox.

"Sign here," she said, handing Mum a tablet and a stylus.

"Thank you." Mum signed the screen.

The driver peered over Mum's shoulder, scanning the hallway. She saw Jarli, but didn't give him a second glance. He didn't look important enough to be the source of the commotion outside. She must not have seen the meme.

"A lot of people out here," the driver said casually.

"Don't ask," Mum told her.

"Well, have a nice day." Suddenly bored, the driver trudged back to her delivery truck, which was five houses away. The news vans hadn't left her anywhere closer to park.

Mum looked at the address label on the package. "It's for you, Jarli."

Jarli trembled. "Why did you take it?"

"What do you mean?"

"It could be anything. It could be a bomb."

Mum sighed. "Jarli—I know you've had a rough night. I have too, believe it or not."

"It could be a bomb," Jarli said again.

"You remember that I work at the post office, right? Every package gets X-rayed and swept with the millimeter wave scanner. Plus, there's the gas chromatograph and the explosive residue test. These days it's impossible to mail a bomb. This feels like"—she squeezed the package, and Jarli winced—"a stuffed toy."

That wasn't a bad guess. Jarli often ordered plush versions of his favorite video game characters. There was something comforting about seeing these huge, menacing creatures reduced to funny collectibles, as helpless and small as he sometimes felt.

Mum tossed the package to Jarli. He jumped back, and it hit the floor next to his feet.

The package didn't explode.

"For goodness' sake, Jarli. It'll be something you ordered. I'll get the police back on the phone—I want them to know about the trolls. Maybe we can get the posts taken down."

Mum walked into the kitchen. Jarli stared at the package. He didn't remember ordering anything lately. He had bought some new headphones, a book, and a new controller, but they'd all arrived. What could this be?

He took the package to his room and got out a pair of scissors. With trembling hands, he sliced through the package and tipped out the object inside.

It was wrapped in tissue paper, but Jarli reluctantly admitted to himself that it didn't look like a bomb. He carefully peeled the paper back.

It was a small, square, satin pillow.

Jarli stared at it, puzzled. He didn't remember ordering anything like that. Maybe there had been a mix-up. He turned the pillow over, looking for an invoice or a receipt.

Then he gasped, and dropped the pillow like it was red-hot.

A message had been carefully embroidered onto the pillow:

Rest in peace, Jarli.

Facing the Wolves

Jarli burst into Dad's room. "We have to move," he said.

Dad sat up, wincing. He'd fallen asleep on top of the covers. He hadn't even taken his shoes off. "What? What's going on?"

Jarli showed him the pillow. "This was just delivered. Someone wants to kill me, and they know where I live."

Dad looked at the pillow for a long time.

"We can't move," he said finally.

"Well, we at least need to leave for a few weeks."

Dad sighed. "Where would we go?"

"Wherever!" Didn't Dad get how urgent this was? "The motel. Aunt Lesley's place. Sydney."

The thing that frightened Jarli most was how quickly the pillow had arrived. The manufacturer was Melbourne-based, but even so, it must have been mailed at least yesterday. After Jarli released his app, but well before the car crash and the televised statement turned him into an international celebrity. Someone had been paying close attention.

"Jarli, listen to me," Dad said. "I know a little bit about this world. I know about shell corporations, decoy accounts, and intermediaries. And I know that a criminal who's planning a murder doesn't send the victim a warning first."

Jarli stared at him. "Are you serious? You're going to bet my life that this is a joke, after what just happened to us?"

"Fine," Dad said. He was starting to sound angry. "Let's assume it's not a joke. This house is surrounded by reporters. Do you really think you'll be safer somewhere else?"

"We could stay with Mr. Gorman," Jarli said. He was the rich owner of a security company. "His house would be secure. And he'd have plenty of space."

"No," Dad said, rubbing his eyes. He had only slept for a couple of hours.

"But he offered," Jarli said. "He said if there was anything he could do—"

"We're not staying with my boss," Dad insisted. "We've imposed on him too much already."

Jarli's phone beeped in the corner. *Lie.* That wasn't the real reason Dad wanted to stay here.

"Are you using your app on me?" Dad demanded.

"I forgot it was on," Jarli mumbled.

"Delete it," Dad said. "Right now."

"No!" Jarli cried.

"Your app has gotten us into enough trouble. Get rid of it."

"If you just trusted me enough to tell me the truth—"

"I don't want you spying on your own family. Delete the app."

Jarli hesitated. If he refused, what would Dad do? Confiscate his phone, probably. And if Jarli wouldn't hand over his phone, Dad would punish him in some other way.

"Fine," Jarli said.

The app beeped. *Lie.* It wasn't fine. In fact, Jarli planned to reinstall it as soon as Dad wasn't watching—but he would have to silence the beeps.

Jarli held up the screen so Dad could see, then he swiped through to the list of apps and stabbed angrily at the screen, making a show of his annoyance. He uninstalled *Truth*.

Now anything anyone told him could be a lie, and he wouldn't know. That hadn't been scary before he made the app. It was scary now. In the two weeks he'd been using the app, he'd become dependent on it. Hopefully he'd be able to reinstall it soon.

Dad held out his hand. "Let me check."

Jarli hesitated. "You saw me delete it."

"I just want to make sure."

Jarli reluctantly handed over his phone. Dad fiddled with it for a while.

"Okay," he said finally. "I'm sorry I doubted you."

Kirstie knocked on the door and walked right in. She had dried her eyes and tied her hair back into a ponytail. "Hey,

Dad," she said, "you know how you crashed our car?"

"It was *my* car," Dad said gloomily, "and that's not exactly what happened."

"Well, how are we going to get to school?"

Jarli checked the old-fashioned alarm clock on Dad's bedside table. It *was* nearly time for school. They'd been up all night.

Dad looked surprised. "You want to go to school?"

Jarli had assumed that they weren't going. But home didn't feel safe anymore, despite what Dad had said. A stranger had been through here, stealing stuff. The house was surrounded by reporters. And a killer—maybe—knew the address.

"Yes," Jarli said.

"But we can't ride our bikes with all those reporters chasing us," Kirstie added. "It would look like the Tour de France."

"I'll call a cab," Jarli said, and walked out before Dad could object.

There was only one taxi company in Kelton, and only four drivers. When the cab pulled up in front of the house, Jarli wasn't surprised to see Bess's mother, Caroline, get out of the driver's seat.

Jarli had known Caroline his whole life. She was one of those "Look how much you've grown!" people—she had gone to college with Mum or something.

Jarli and Kirstie didn't wait for her to push through the crowd to the front door. They ran out of the house, carrying their school bags and wearing sunglasses.

The reporters rushed in, stabbing at Jarli with microphones and blocking his view with bulky video cameras. Every camera flash felt like an electric shock.

"Jarli! Do you regret making the app?"

"How do you feel about other people making money from your work?"

"How would you describe your performance in yesterday's interview?"

Jarli kept his mouth clamped shut. He and Kirstie forced their way through the crowd toward the taxi. Soon Jarli realized that the reporters blocking his path weren't actually allowed to touch him. If he kept walking forward, they would have to move out of the way.

Caroline was holding the back door open for them. Jarli had never seen her look so cheerful. Her uniform was neatly pressed, and her usually frizzy hair was covered by a shiny cap. She owned the taxi company, and she must have decided that this was a publicity opportunity.

Jarli and Kirstie scrambled inside. Caroline closed the door and circled back around to the driver's side. She waved to the crowd of reporters before climbing in.

"Hi, Mrs. Deshara," Jarli said.

"Hey, Caroline," Kirstie said at the same moment.

"Hey, kids," Caroline said. "Going to school?"

"Yep."

"That'll be about twenty dollars. Do you have enough money for this journey?"

"Of course we do," Jarli said, offended. "Why would you ask us that?"

"New policy." Caroline beamed. "I've distributed your app to all my drivers. They ask every passenger if they have enough cash, and the app tells them if the passenger is lying. It's going to save me a lot of money."

"Glad I could help," Jarli said. At least someone appreciated his work.

Caroline pulled away from the curb and drove carefully between the parked news vans. "Of course, you guys can ride for free today. That footage of you getting into my cab is a great ad for the company."

"But you're the only taxi company in Kelton," Jarli said. "Why do you need to advertise?"

"Shut up, Jarli!" Kirstie hissed. "She's giving us a free ride!"

"I have plenty of competitors," Caroline said. "Buses. Bicycles. Privately owned cars. Legs. Trust me, the advertising helps."

"Where's Bess?" Jarli asked. Caroline usually dropped her off at school.

"She decided to catch the bus today," Caroline said.

Her phone was on the seat next to her. The screen flashed orange. *Half truth.*

"Okay, I *told* her to take the bus," Caroline admitted. "I thought with all the reporters, she might get self-conscious about her crutches."

Bess was never shy about her crutches, but Jarli knew that other people got embarrassed on her behalf. The phone didn't react to this statement, so Caroline at least thought she was telling the truth.

"Your phone flashed orange," Jarli said. "I didn't program the app to do that."

"I'm using the paid version of your app," Caroline said.

"Paid version?"

"Yeah. The description said it works on text messages and e-mails, not just speech—is that right?"

Jarli got out his phone and searched the list of available apps. There it was: *Truth Premium,* right next to his own app. Someone had copied *Truth* and was selling it. More than fifty thousand people had downloaded it so far.

"I should sue somebody," he muttered.

Caroline didn't hear him. "I like the way it matches people to their social media profiles and keeps a record of how honest each person is in general."

Jarli tried to download the app. He hated giving these people his money, but he wanted to see how it worked.

A message popped up.

Password required

Jarli frowned. That didn't usually happen when he tried to download apps. He put his usual password in. The phone beeped angrily.

Login Failed

Dad must have gone into the settings and added a new password so Jarli couldn't reinstall his app.

Jarli was furious, but he knew he didn't really have the right to be angry at Dad. He'd tricked Jarli, but Jarli had tried to trick him first. So he diverted his anger toward the people who had ripped off his app instead.

"If it's judging text messages and e-mails, it won't be accurate," Jarli complained. "It can't hear the person's voice or see their face. It'll be wrong twenty percent of the time."

Caroline shrugged. "Doesn't bother me. My drivers will be quizzing people in person."

Kirstie grinned. "Are you a bit jealous, Jarli?"

"It's irresponsible," Jarli grumbled.

Kirstie's phone beeped. She must have installed the paid app already.

She looked at the screen. "Reframing," she announced. "You avoided answering the question. According to this, you're only sixty-six percent honest."

"What?" Jarli snatched the phone out of her hand. It was true. There was his profile picture from social media, and an honesty score.

"Some of the reporters from last night must have been using the paid version," Kirstie said. "I figure the app has only heard you say six things, and two of them weren't true. Give me my phone back."

Jarli handed it over and hugged his knees. This was a nightmare. He had a new reputation for dishonesty, someone else was making money off his work, everyone on the Internet thought he was stupid, and someone was trying to kill him.

"Feet off seats!" Caroline said.

Jarli put his legs down. "Sorry," he muttered.

Kirstie's phone beeped. *Lie.* Jarli wasn't sorry. On the screen, his honesty score dipped to 57 percent. Soon no one would ever trust him again.

Hunted

When Jarli got out of the taxi, all the people in front of Kelton High School fell silent. Dozens of students, huddled in groups, stared at him. Their parents paused halfway back to their cars. A couple of teachers shot Jarli hostile looks.

Yesterday, Jarli had been invisible. Today he was the center of attention. It didn't feel as good as he had hoped.

"If anyone asks," Kirstie said, "we're not related."

"Thanks for your support," Jarli said.

There were a few reporters here, but not many, and none had cameras. There was some kind of rule about not showing the faces of children without their parents' permission. Jarli wasn't sure why this rule protected the other students and not him, but at least the reporters couldn't step onto the school grounds. It was as though a spell kept them behind an invisible wall. When they saw Jarli they started yelling questions. Jarli ignored them as he shuffled toward the school.

It was a sandstone building in the corner of a dusty field bordering some drought-hardened bushland. On winter mornings, Weirwalla Hill would cast a shadow across the school, but not now. The sun was already uncomfortably hot.

Kirstie had once described the building as "like an Egyptian pyramid, only it's a cube." This statement sounded silly—the main feature of a pyramid was that it *wasn't* a cube—but that didn't stop it from being true. The school seemed to be ancient, the hard edges worn away by centuries of harsh winds.

The students had started whispering. "You see the interview?"

"What interview?"

"Oh man! You gotta check this out."

A girl pulled out her phone and showed the boy next to her. Jarli didn't need to see the screen to know what they were watching. His face hot, he pushed through the crowd toward the doors.

A nasty surprise was waiting for him inside. Someone had printed out dozens of photos and glued them to his locker. All the photos were the same—a screenshot from Jarli's TV interview. On the page, Jarli looked sweaty and hollow-eyed. The picture was captioned: NO MORE QUESTIONS!

Jarli could feel people staring at him as he tried to peel the pictures off. It was no use. They were printed on cheap paper that was weaker than the glue. He could only tear off tiny strips.

Another boy, Owen, was walking past. Jarli knew him from

the Coders Club, which met in the library on Mondays. Owen always had a steel ruler in his pencil case—maybe Jarli could use it to scrape off the posters.

"Hey, Owen," Jarli said. "Got a sec?"

Owen kept walking as though he hadn't heard.

"Hello? Earth to Owen." Jarli grabbed Owen's shoulder.

Owen shook off Jarli's hand. "I can't help you," he mumbled without making eye contact. Then he scurried away, keeping his head down until he was out of sight.

Jarli couldn't believe it. He had helped Owen test games. They were supposed to be friends. Giving up on the posters, Jarli opened the locker, and recoiled as a foul smell wafted out. Someone had pushed a squishy brown substance through the ventilation holes, covering his library books. Jarli told himself that it was rotten fruit, but it could easily have been cow poo from the school's agricultural plot.

He would have to clean it up later. The smell was making him dizzy. His head started to throb and the edges of his vision went black. A migraine was coming on. He should have stayed home.

The bell rang. Jarli closed the locker without taking anything out. He turned to go to class, wondering how he would explain his lack of writing materials to the teacher. . . .

But he found his path blocked. Four students were standing in the way, arms folded. Two boys, two girls.

Behind him, Jarli found six more kids barring the way.

Some were older than Jarli, some were a bit younger. He was surrounded. A few of the kids were holding up their phones, shooting video.

One of them was Doug Hennessey.

Doug had moved to Kelton last year. He was in most of Jarli's classes, and he always sat near the back of the room, radiating anger. It was as though there was a big snake in the corner, and everyone was just pretending it wasn't there. Jarli had never heard him say a single word.

Now he said, "Jarli Durras. We want to talk to you."

"About what?" Jarli said warily.

A boy with a half-shaved eyebrow spoke up. "My dad used your app on me," he said. "Now I'm not allowed to leave the house."

"Maybe you shouldn't have lied to your dad," Jarli said. His head was still pounding. He looked around for a teacher, but there were none to be seen.

"My honesty score is forty percent," said a boy with bangs that covered half his face. "Now no one trusts me."

"That's not even my app," Jarli said, getting angry. "Someone else copied me."

"Mum took away my phone," said a girl with dyed-black hair and zip-up boots. "I hadn't even done anything wrong—she was just afraid that I would use your app on her."

"That's your mum's fault, not mine."

Doug didn't say what he had been caught for. Maybe he

didn't want the others to know. Instead he said, "You shouldn't have made that app. Actions have consequences."

It was almost exactly what Jarli's mother had said, but now it sounded like a threat.

"If you lied about something and got caught," Jarli said, "that's on you."

Doug turned purple with rage. Whatever had happened to him, it was something bad.

"Get him!" he snarled.

As the wall of kids rushed inward, Jarli darted sideways, trying to squeeze between them and the lockers. But he was still dizzy. He tripped and slammed down onto the floor. He wondered if someone had stuck their foot out as his body bounced on the linoleum.

As the world went dark, Mum's voice echoed through his head. *Did it not occur to you that almost everyone has secrets?*

How many more people would be out to get Jarli?

The Veteran

I t's not broken," the school nurse said. "But you're going to
have a nasty bruise."

Jarli hardly ever got sick. During flu season everyone
else in his family would take a couple of days off school or
work, but not him. And he hardly ever got injured, because
running was his only sport. He didn't get grazed knees like
the basketball players, or concussions like the football team.

So when he woke up on the floor of the empty corridor,
his wrist aching, he didn't know where the infirmary was. He
wandered through the school for ages before he found it. The
entrance turned out to be inside the school gym, which made
sense—that would be where most of the injuries happened.

In the infirmary, the fluorescent lights hurt his eyes. The
first-aid posters on the walls took a while to come into focus.
His head throbbed. He was so tired.

"Here." The nurse had an ice pack wrapped in a washcloth.
She pressed it against Jarli's wrist. She was a middle-aged
woman in capri pants and a gray turtleneck. She had a kind
smile but sad eyes. Her name was Maria Eaton.

"You want to tell me what happened?" she asked.

Jarli shook his head.

Eaton took the ice pack off and examined Jarli's wrist for a moment, then she put it back on. "You know," she said, "I used to be a surgeon in the army. One of the units I worked with—"

"Really? How did you end up here?"

"I finished my tour and quit."

"Aren't you overqualified for this job?"

"Yes." Eaton didn't elaborate. "Anyway, my unit had this old guy—actually he was only thirty-seven, but the other soldiers were all in their twenties, so he seemed old to them. They called him Nursing Home. They played pranks on him, made jokes about how he couldn't keep up. And they outranked him—he was just a private."

Leaving Jarli with the ice pack, she went over to the sink and scrubbed her hands.

"I treated him more than anyone else in that unit," she continued. "Mostly bruises, some grazes. I realized pretty quickly that the other soldiers were responsible. But he never complained. If he'd told his commanding officer, the bullying might have stopped."

Jarli remembered the hostile looks from the teachers this morning. They, too, might have secrets that were threatened by the app. He wasn't convinced they would help him.

"Here." Nurse Eaton handed him a plastic cup of water

and glanced down as his file. "Are you allergic to acetaminophen?"

"No."

"Okay. Swallow this and drink all the water." Eaton handed Jarli a tablet. Jarli gulped it down.

"What happened to the old guy in your unit?" Jarli asked. "Nursing Home?"

"They left him behind during a retreat," Eaton said. "He's dead."

Jarli walked out of the infirmary and onto the dusty wooden floor of the gym. Bess was sitting nearby on an equipment crate. Her crutches were balanced on her lap and she was trying, and failing, to spin a basketball on one finger. Jarli had never been so relieved to see her.

"Bess," he said. "Shouldn't you be in class?"

"Nah, stuff that." Bess put the ball down and brushed her long, dark hair out of her eyes. "My best friend needs me."

Whenever Jarli was in some kind of trouble—if he was struggling with an assignment, or he'd been "too honest" with another student—Bess was usually the one who helped him out.

"I don't think you can fix this," Jarli said gloomily.

"I have music class, so I may as well try." Bess was always looking for an excuse to get out of music class because she never did any practice at home. Her parents thought playing the trumpet would be good for her brain, but she struggled to move her fingers fast enough.

Bess and Jarli had been friends since they were kids. They often helped each other with projects—he had sorted out the domain registration for her blog, and she had been the first and only special guest on his podcast. Jarli knew her so well that he hadn't even been able to test his app with her. They had tried lying to each other, and the app didn't pick it up. This could have been because they weren't nervous, or maybe because they didn't actually intend to deceive each other.

Jarli sat down next to her. "Well, I'm glad to see you. Did you catch my TV interview?"

"Yeah. Don't be too hard on yourself. I've seen politicians do just as badly."

It took Jarli a few minutes to tell Bess about the robbery and explain all the other things that hadn't fit into his messages. Bess listened, wide-eyed.

"So you think the old man broke into your house?" she asked when he was finished.

Jarli hesitated. That hadn't occurred to him.

"Why would he do that?" he asked.

"I don't know, but if it wasn't him, it's a pretty weird coincidence. Since he couldn't kill you, maybe he decided to steal your stuff instead."

"That doesn't make much sense." Jarli squeezed his skull

between his palms. "Then again, nothing seems to make sense anymore."

Bess patted him on the back. "Hey, at least there's a bright side."

"What?"

"Mr. Kendrick got fired."

"*What?*"

Bess smirked. "Yup. His diploma was a forgery. He's not qualified to teach. And it was your app that busted him! He was saying something about his time at college, and everyone's phones went off."

"Huh." Jarli had never liked Kendrick, who shouted at students for no good reason and often criticized their work in front of the class. He also tried his hardest to get Jarli expelled after he found out that Jarli had hacked into his e-mail account. But Jarli didn't feel good about him getting fired.

"How's your wrist, anyway?" Bess asked.

"Sore. But Nurse Eaton says it'll be okay."

"Did she tell you one of her war stories?" Bess asked.

Jarli laughed. "Yeah. Does she do that a lot?"

"Every time I go in," Bess said. "I think she's making it all up. Why would a combat surgeon end up as a school nurse in Kelton? Use your app on her next time—see if she's telling the truth."

"Dad made me uninstall my own app," Jarli grumbled.

"Then he password-protected my phone so I couldn't put it back on."

"Seriously?" Bess shifted her weight on the equipment crate. "That probably makes you the only person on Earth now who isn't using the app."

"Are *you* using it?"

"I had to turn it off. It kept telling me people were lying to me."

"That's the point," Jarli said.

"I know. But sometimes I'd rather believe what people are saying."

"You're as bad as my sister." Jarli shut his eyes, willing the throbbing in his head to go away.

"Don't worry about the old man—or anyone else. From now on, I'm your personal bodyguard." Bess hefted one of her crutches. "You'd be amazed how hard I can swing these things."

"Thanks, Bess."

"Are you going to class?"

"No. I think I'll call your mum and get a ride home."

"Well, give her plenty of warning. She'll want to do her hair and makeup for the cameras. She might even want to put out a press release titled: *Nation's Best Taxi Service Drives Local Celebrity.*"

"She is *loving* this, isn't she?"

"Little bit, yeah."

They sat in silence for a moment.

The gym doors opened. Jarli turned to look.

Anya was standing in the doorway.

"Jarli," she gasped. "There's a brown truck parked behind the school!"

Incursion

Jarli's heart kicked into overdrive. At first he hoped it was a prank. Maybe Anya's life had been ruined by the app, and she hated him too.

But she looked deadly serious. Her cheeks were red and her hair was a mess. She had sprinted here to give him this message.

"Did you see the old man?" he asked.

"No. The truck was empty." Anya ran in, letting the door fall closed behind her.

It took Jarli a moment to realize what this meant. The old man must be somewhere *in the school*, searching for him!

All the color had drained from Bess's face. She pulled out her phone. "I'll call the police."

"It will take them a while to get here," Anya said. "We have to get you off the school grounds."

Jarli hesitated. If he wasn't at school, wouldn't he be even more exposed? Maybe he should find somewhere to hide instead.

"Police," Bess was saying. "A man is here looking for

my friend. He's dangerous. We're at Kelton High School."

Jarli knocked on the infirmary door and pushed it open without waiting for an answer. "Miss Eaton," he said. "There's a—"

He broke off. The infirmary was empty. The nurse was gone.

Jarli looked around, baffled. There were no other doors. Had she slipped past them somehow?

He looked at the window, wondering if she had gone out that way for some reason. But what he saw through the glass was a tall figure, carrying a bucket of cleaning supplies, walking toward the gym.

The old man was coming!

The panic hit Jarli like a wrecking ball. He ducked out of sight and scrambled back through the open door into the gym.

"He's here!" he whispered. "What do we do?"

"Please hurry!" Bess hissed into the phone.

Anya ripped open the equipment crate and grabbed a tennis racket. She sprinted back to the gym door and jammed the racket through the handles so the door couldn't be opened.

She acted just in time. Footsteps crunched toward the outside of the door. The handles rattled.

Jarli held his breath.

There was a knock at the door.

The three kids looked at one another, eyes wide.

"Who is it?" Bess yelled.

"This building is scheduled for cleaning," a voice said. "You kids shouldn't be in there."

"We're doing an exam," Bess said. "We're not supposed to be interrupted."

Looking at Jarli, she mouthed, *Go! We'll distract him.* She pointed at the window in the infirmary.

"What about you guys?" Jarli whispered. He couldn't leave them to face the old man alone.

"He's after you, not us," Bess replied. "Go!"

"The principal said it was urgent," the old man was saying through the door. "I won't distract you."

"It's a make-up exam," Bess shouted. "We aren't allowed to let anyone in until it's done."

Jarli ran into the infirmary, closed the door, and went to the window. He looked around the frame for a latch, but there wasn't one. How had Nurse Eaton gotten out?

There was no time to fiddle around. He needed to get out of here, now. Jarli ripped the blankets off the bed and held them up against the glass. With his other hand he grabbed a paperweight off the desk—it was a lump of metal shaped like a set of scales.

Jarli had never broken a window before. His first tap was too timid. The glass didn't break.

He whacked it again, harder.

This time the glass splintered. Even through the blanket,

the crack was loud. Jarli cringed as broken pieces jingled against the concrete outside.

He draped the blanket over the window frame so he could climb through without cutting his hands. His shoes crunched across the broken glass outside, and then he was sprinting across the sports field toward the bushland.

There was no fence at the school perimeter. The vegetation was thick and deep, all the way up to Weirwalla Hill. The old man would never find him in there. But Jarli was still worried about Bess and Anya.

When he was almost at the other end of the sports field, he snatched a glance back. There was no sign of the police yet. Jarli could see the old man, standing outside the gymnasium. He was pounding on the door, yelling something.

Then he seemed to sense that someone was looking at him. He turned his head and saw Jarli.

They stared at each other for a moment, about fifty meters apart.

The old man reached into his bucket and pulled out a gun.

Faster Than a Bullet

Jarli fled into the bush. The fear made him sprint faster than ever before. It felt like his feet hardly touched the ground.

Something whizzed past his ear. A split second later Jarli heard the crack of a gunshot. He screamed and kept running for his life.

He ran uphill, swerving left and right at random, ducking around trees and rocks. He wished he could turn around and get back to the school or the town, where other people might protect him. But the old man was close behind—Jarli could hear him crashing through the scrub. His only option was to get out of sight.

Bang! Another gunshot. Jarli barged through a cluster of bushes, darted right and kept running.

He risked a look behind him as he went over a fence, then up a short winding trail. He couldn't see the old man. Maybe the old man couldn't see him either. But there were no hiding places here. He had to keep moving.

Jarli turned his head forward just in time to see that he was running toward the edge of a cliff.

He stopped so fast that his shoes slid out from under him. He landed on his back and sprawled on the smooth rocks, legs dangling off the edge.

He was facing the Weirwalla falls. The waterfall itself had dried up over the hot summer, but there was still a deep pool of water far below. It was a thirty-six-foot drop—Jarli knew that because it had been in the news last year. Some guy had needed to be rescued after he jumped off. He'd broken his ankle when he hit the water. Since then, the top of the waterfall had been fenced and closed to the public, although the school still held swimming classes in the lake below.

He scrambled to his feet and ran along the cliff's edge. There was a squat boulder up ahead—he ducked behind it, breathing hard.

It wasn't big enough. If the old man walked past, he would see Jarli. This wasn't a great hiding place. Jarli scanned his surroundings for a better one.

There! A hole in the ground a little farther up the hill, like someone had removed one of the big rocks that made up the cliff's top. Jarli couldn't tell how deep the hole was. Hopefully there would be enough space to hide in.

He scrambled out from behind the boulder. He was exposed for four strides, and then he dropped into the hole, heart thundering. It was a tight fit. He had to bunch himself up into a tiny ball to get his head below the top.

Footsteps crunched on the rocks nearby. Jarli held his

breath. He was shaking so much that he worried the old man would hear his skeleton rattling.

The footsteps moved closer and closer to the hole. A shadow fell across Jarli—

And then the footsteps moved away, farther up the hill. The old man hadn't seen him.

Jarli waited until he couldn't hear the footsteps anymore. Then he got out his phone and called 911. The phone rang and rang.

Eventually someone picked up. There was no hello. Just four words: "Fire, police, or ambulance?"

"Police," Jarli whispered.

"Fire, police, or ambulance?" the woman repeated. She hadn't heard him.

"Police!" Jarli hissed, a little louder. "Hurry! I'm being—"

"Putting you through now," the woman said. The phone started ringing again.

Jarli listened. The footsteps were coming back. Faster this time. The old man must have heard Jarli talking.

"Police," a gruff voice said. But Jarli couldn't reply—he had to run before the old man got any closer. If he found Jarli in this hole, it would be like shooting fish in a barrel. Even easier, because this fish was so big that it could hardly fit in the barrel.

Jarli scrambled out of the hole and started running downhill—

Then he saw the old man, climbing up the slope toward him. Jarli had gone the wrong way!

The old man spotted Jarli and picked up the pace. Jarli was trapped at edge of the cliff, thirty-six feet above the water. The trees were too far away to provide any cover. If he turned to run, he would be shot in the back.

The old man was now so close that he couldn't miss. He raised his pistol and took aim at Jarli.

So Jarli jumped off the cliff.

Cornered

Ten Minutes Earlier

The infirmary door was closed, but Anya heard Jarli smash the window. He was making too much noise. Surely the old man would hear.

But no. The old man started pounding on the door instead.

"Don't make me break this door down," he snarled. "You have ten seconds. Ten. Nine."

Anya and Bess looked at each other, terrified. The old man seemed to have dropped the pretense that he was just a cleaner.

"We've called the police," Anya called. "Soon they'll have the school surrounded."

"Six," the old man was saying. "Five."

"How strong do you think that door is?" Bess whispered.

"Not strong enough," Anya said.

"Three," the old man said. "Two."

And then there was silence.

Anya and Bess backed away from the door, but there was

no more noise from outside. Maybe he was gone—or he wanted them to think he was.

"He's trying to scare us," Anya whispered. "Or confuse us."

"It's working!" Bess hissed.

Bang! Anya jumped as the gunshot rang out. She ducked, but there were no holes in the door. The old man must have been shooting at someone else.

She ran over to the door and grabbed the tennis racket that was jammed through the handles.

"What are you doing?" Bess demanded.

Anya wrenched the racket free, unlocking the door. "He's spotted Jarli," she said. "We have to help him."

She pulled the doors open and stepped out into the daylight, just in time to see the old man run into the bushland and disappear.

Anya looked around, but there was no sign of the police, or a teacher, or anyone else who might be chasing him. And his car had been around the other side of the building, so he wasn't leaving in that.

That meant he was probably chasing Jarli.

"Stay here," Anya told Bess. "Tell the police what's going on when they get here."

"Where are you going?" Bess asked.

Anya was already running toward the forest. If Jarli was on his own out there, he didn't stand a chance.

She had hoped to be able to follow the old man's footprints, or Jarli's. But it was no good. The ground was hard and dry. She had no hope of finding either trail.

Bang! A second gunshot. The echoes bounced around confusingly, seeming to come from everywhere at once—but Anya saw a flock of startled birds take flight farther up the hill. That was where the old man had fired from. Anya scurried up the trail, keeping her head down. Soon she could hear the old man trampling the shrubbery.

As she got closer, she slowed down. She couldn't hear any more gunshots or voices. The old man might have lost sight of Jarli—Anya didn't want his crosshairs to settle on her instead.

She crept up and up, careful not to step on any dry twigs or rattle any leafy branches.

She paused as she heard footsteps ahead. They sounded light and quick. Jarli, maybe?

Anya parted the leaves in time to see Jarli jump off the cliff.

Free Fall

The gun went off a split second after Jarli jumped. The bullet just missed his chest and skipped off a rock on the other side of the ravine. Gun smoke burned his nostrils.

For a split second it was strangely peaceful, hanging in the air, staring out at the trees on the horizon. Then Jarli looked down at the distant water and started to fall. It was as if glancing down had made gravity notice him, like in an old cartoon.

At first it was just like falling from the monkey bars or jumping off the swings. But then he kept accelerating, faster and faster, his organs swimming, his head spinning, his heartbeat in his ears. The air blasted his face and made cushions under his hands. He spread his arms and legs wide like a skydiver, trying to slow himself down. It didn't help. Jarli suddenly realized that he was screaming.

There was a deafening crack as the old man took another shot at him. Jarli cringed, but it missed. Then the water rushed up to meet him like an oncoming train. He squeezed his eyes shut.

Wham! Jarli crashed down into the water, feet first. He felt a sudden shock of agony through his whole body. There was a tearing sensation in his armpits and hamstrings. Suddenly Jarli was under the brown water, blind and deaf. His clothes immediately became heavy and tight.

With a dull thump, his throbbing feet hit the bottom of the lake.

Jarli desperately wanted to push back up to the surface but his limbs wouldn't obey him. It was as though the nerves that controlled them had burned out. In any case, the old man would see him, and take another shot. So he waited for the feeling in his limbs to return, crouched at the bottom of the muddy lake, his eyes shut, his lungs ready to burst. This far down, the pressure was crushing. His eardrums ached. He forced himself to count to ten, then twenty.

Soon Jarli couldn't take it any longer. He launched himself off the bottom of the lake. The movement hurt every muscle in his body, but at least they obeyed, and none of his limbs bent in funny directions. He hadn't broken any bones.

Jarli rose up, up, up through the water. His chest was on fire. With each stroke of his arm, he kept expecting to break through the surface. But there was always more water above him.

Don't breathe in, he thought to himself. *No matter how much you want to. You'll drown. Come on, Jarli. Just a little bit farther.*

But at that moment he knew he'd waited too long. Without oxygen, his vision started to waver. He was going to black out.

Then his head emerged from the water.

He wanted a deep gasp of air. But the old man could be watching and listening. Instead, Jarli made himself take shallow breaths through his nose as he floated on his back. It was so hard to control his relief, and his chest was still crying out for a giant lungful of air, not just tiny sniffs, but he kept his eyes closed and his mouth slightly open. He spread his arms and legs wide to stay buoyant. Hopefully, if the old man was still up there he would think Jarli was dead.

But maybe the old man would take aim at the floating body and shoot, just to be sure.

Jarli tried to keep his breaths slow and gentle, forcing himself not to panic. Nothing happened for a long time. The cold water, still rippling from Jarli's crash-landing, lapped gently at the sides of his face. Birds whistled in the distant trees.

He opened his eyes just a crack, peering through his eyelashes. No one was on the cliff's top. The old man had gone.

Jarli moved one arm and, inch by inch, his floating body slowly rotated. Now he could see the water's edge. No one was there either.

Jarli swam quietly toward the shore and crawled onto dry land. His body hurt too much to stand. But he was alive. He had survived a third encounter with the old man. Jarli got the feeling that he wouldn't be so lucky a fourth time.

He dug his phone out of his pocket. It wouldn't switch on. The water had killed it.

He had to get back to civilization as soon as possible. The old man might still be nearby, and this time Anya and Bess could back up his story. The cops would have to believe Jarli now. And the sooner they started the search, the better their chances of catching the old man.

Jarli gingerly trudged up the muddy shore toward the trees where a narrow path led back to Kelton. His muscles ached. His wet, sandy clothes rubbed his skin raw. His soaked shoes were as heavy as full cartons of milk. Every step drove shards of pain into his feet.

The trees loomed on either side, as close and intimidating as the reporters had been. Was the car crash only last night? It felt as though he'd aged since then. Like his body thought he was going to die, and was trying to become as old as possible before it happened.

This must be how Dad had felt after the car crash. Jarli felt a stab of guilt. If the old man was targeting Jarli because of the app, then the crash was Jarli's fault. He had nearly gotten his father killed.

A stick snapped somewhere up ahead.

Jarli froze. He heard footsteps approaching.

No, no, no! Had Jarli been through all this for nothing? He scrambled into the bushes and crouched down. He couldn't run away. He was too tired, too sore. If the old man spotted him, he was doomed.

The footsteps crunched closer and closer. Jarli kept perfectly still, eyes shut. With all the mud covering his clothes, he probably looked like a rock. He tried to imagine that he *was* a rock, fearless and invincible.

A hand grabbed his shoulder.

Alone

Anya thought Jarli might be dead.

She had been up here once before. She had seen the height of that cliff. And she knew from science class that water was incompressible—landing on it was like landing on concrete, except that concrete doesn't swallow you afterward.

Could she have saved him? If she had gotten up here faster, instead of moving cautiously, she could have charged at the old man before Jarli jumped. Maybe they could have overpowered him together. Or maybe she and Jarli both would have gotten shot.

It was too late now. Jarli was gone. Anya was on her own.

She watched the old man peer over the cliff's edge. Then he turned around in a slow circle, scanning the bush. His face was impossible to read. He didn't look pleased, or frustrated, or suspicious. He may as well have been a robot.

Anya wished her clothes were green, to blend in. But she was wearing the bright blue uniform of Kelton High School. If the old man's eyes were good, he would spot her. She stayed perfectly still in the bushes.

Something smooth and soft touched her fingers.

She glanced down and saw a fat brown snake, slowly slithering across the back of her hand. She clamped her mouth closed, but couldn't suppress a terrified squeak.

Humans rarely frightened Anya. They were predictable. Anya didn't need Jarli's app—she could usually see what people were thinking. Her parents hadn't spoken much English when they moved here, so Anya had learned the language slowly. Since the words often eluded her, she had gotten very good at reading faces and bodies. Even in boxing, she always knew what her opponent intended to do. Their eyes gave them away.

Not snakes, though. Everything about them was mysterious. The way they moved, their forked tongues, their slitted pupils, and their upside-down eyelids. This snake could decide to bite her at any moment, without warning.

She couldn't move without revealing her position to the old man. So she stayed frozen, watching as the snake slid over her hand and pooled in the dirt on the other side.

It stayed there a moment, tasting the air. Then, with an unreadable glance at Anya, it poured itself away into the bushes.

When it was gone, Anya stopped holding her breath. Heart pounding, she glanced back up at the old man.

He was gone.

Anya looked around. Where was he?

A parrot launched itself out of the shrubbery somewhere to her right, flapping and squawking. Anya turned to look—

And saw the old man creeping toward her. He had spotted Anya, and was trying to sneak up on her!

Anya broke cover and ran, sprinting down the hill toward the school. She avoided the narrow trail, instead crashing through the undergrowth, leaping over fallen trees, and ducking under low-hanging branches. The old man was big. She would use this to her advantage.

The old man's boots were snapping twigs and crushing leaves behind her. It sounded like he was falling behind. But what if he decided to take a shot?

She turned her head to see how far behind he was.

The old man was a long way back, marching through the forest like a clockwork soldier. Soon he would be out of sight—

But then Anya tripped on a hidden tree root.

Her legs slipped out from under her and suddenly she was hurtling sideways. She flung her arms out, trying to grab hold of something, anything. But her hands gripped empty air. She had a split-second view of a tree trunk rushing toward her head. Heart racing, she tried to cover her face with her arms—

THUMP. Anya was unconscious before she hit the dirt.

Rescued

Jarli tried to wriggle free, but the hand was too strong.

"Help!" he screamed.

Someone held him down, but gently. "Easy," a voice said. "Easy."

The voice was female. Jarli stopped struggling, and twisted his head. It was Constable Blanco, the cop with the chipped tooth.

"Are you hurt?" she said.

Jarli opened his mouth, but no words came out. He'd been through too much. Tears stung the corners of his eyes.

"Bess told us about the old man," Blanco said. "Is he nearby?"

"I don't know," Jarli whispered.

Blanco took in their surroundings, checking the trees and scrub. Birds chirruped. Insects hummed back and forth.

"Come with me," Blanco said finally. "Can you walk?"

Jarli tried, but his legs wobbled beneath him like stilts. Blanco caught him as he fell.

Bess feels like this all the time, Jarli thought. He realized he didn't know where Bess was, or if she was okay. She was his best friend, and he'd just left her at the school. What if the old man had gone back there? What if—

Blanco wrapped one arm around his rib cage, ignoring the mud smearing her uniform, and helped Jarli walk up the trail. He put his arm around her neck, too exhausted to be embarrassed.

The bush fell quiet around them. Jarli couldn't see the old man, but he still had a sense of being watched.

Blanco felt it too. "Hurry," she whispered. She touched the radio on her shoulder.

"Frink," she said. "You there?"

The radio crackled. *"Yup."*

"I'm inbound with a witness. Keep searching."

"Copy that," Constable Frink said.

Soon Jarli saw some flashing lights through the trees. Blanco's patrol car was parked off the nearest road. Blanco helped Jarli into the back seat. "Watch your head. There's some paper towels back there if you want to get yourself cleaned up."

Jarli barely heard her. He was just relieved that someone else had taken charge. The police knew about the old man now—it wasn't Jarli's problem anymore. He buckled himself in and immediately fell asleep.

He woke up to find the police car surrounded by reporters. For a moment he wasn't sure what was real—maybe he was on his way home from the hospital, and the cliff and the lake had been a dream.

But the mud on his clothes was very real. And this wasn't Gorman's car. There was steel mesh between Jarli and the driver.

Blanco muttered something obscene and then wound down the window. "All right, you vultures," she said. "You know the rules. Get back, before I have you all arrested."

Grumbling, the photographers backed off. Jarli felt a rush of gratitude. He wondered if Blanco would come back to his house for a while. His family would be safe with her around.

Blanco opened the door and helped Jarli out of the car. Some reporters shouted questions, but Jarli couldn't work out what they were. His ears still had water in them.

Jarli had never been inside the Kelton police station. The entrance was a little bit like a doctor's waiting room, with a stack of old magazines in one corner and children's toys in another. But there was no carpet and all the chairs were bolted to the floor, as though officers were worried that someone might steal one.

The pile of toys made Jarli sad. He wondered how many little kids ended up in here, waiting for the cops to finish with mum or dad.

The receptionist gave Blanco a form, and she filled it in quickly. Then she took Jarli to an interview room that smelled like bleach and smoke. There were four chairs around a big table and a security camera in the corner. Jarli had expected there to be one-way glass, but there wasn't.

"Take a seat," Blanco said. "Can I get you a tea or coffee? Hot chocolate?"

Jarli suddenly realized how thirsty he was. The back of his throat tasted like blood, as if he'd just run a marathon.

"Water," he rasped. "Thanks."

Blanco nodded. "Be right back."

Before she left, she patted him gently on the shoulder. Jarli wondered if she felt guilty about not believing him earlier. He was too tired to be angry about that.

Blanco let the door fall closed behind her.

Jarli sat down in one of the metal chairs. There was no cushioning. It was the sort of chair a person could be handcuffed to. He still felt like he might fall asleep in it.

The door opened. It wasn't Blanco. It was the receptionist—a man with a thick mustache and a receding hairline. He was holding a cell phone.

"You left your phone in reception," he told Jarli.

"That's not mine," Jarli said.

"You're Jarli, right?"

"Yeah."

The receptionist held out the phone. "Your dad's on the line. Says he couldn't get through to your other phone."

Confused, Jarli took the phone. The receptionist left the room.

Jarli put the phone to his ear. "Dad," he said. "Don't worry, I'm okay."

"No, you're not. You're in deep trouble."

Goose bumps prickled the back of Jarli's neck. That wasn't Dad's voice. It was a deep, rough, gurgly voice. The old man.

"You're going to do exactly what I tell you," the man continued. "Or Anya dies."

Hostage

Anya woke up in the trunk of a car.

The smell of diesel was overpowering, and the engine noise seemed to make the air shake. The car was moving, fast. Anya wasn't sure how she had gotten there. One minute she had been running through the forest, and then . . . nothing. Blackness.

She felt cold metal on her wrist. It had been handcuffed to her ankle, making it hard to move. There was a sort of antiseptic sting in her nostrils—maybe he had chloroformed her, like in the movies.

"Help!" she screamed. "Help me! Somebody!" She pounded the lid of the trunk with her free arm.

The driver didn't stop or change direction or speed up. He wasn't worried about anyone hearing her. The car was probably on a highway, where there were no pedestrians.

She felt in her pocket for her phone. Gone.

Anya started counting the seconds. Not just to calm herself down—the cops would want to know how far she had traveled. *One. Two. Three.*

When she got to nine hundred and twelve, the car abruptly changed direction. It rolled over some rough terrain and eventually ground to a stop.

A door thumped. Footsteps crunched around the car. The trunk popped open and light flooded in.

Anya was still blinking when the old man hauled her out and dropped her on the gravel.

"Move," he said. "That way."

She stood up awkwardly, one arm behind her back. If it hadn't been for the handcuffs, Anya could have dealt with him. Yes, he was big, but she could have made that his weakness rather than his strength. At boxing, her partners were usually bigger than her. She had learned to use their weight against them.

But with one hand attached to her ankle, there was nothing she could do. She was as helpless as a flamingo, standing on one foot. So she hopped in the direction he was pointing.

They were on a dirt road surrounded by dense bushland. A warehouse, painted green and gray to match the foliage, was visible through the trees.

When Anya reached the warehouse, the old man grabbed her and put a bag on her head.

The bag had no handles and was made of heavy black fabric. Anya concluded that it was *designed* to go on people's heads. Her captor was a professional.

This could be good or bad. A professional was less likely

to kill her by accident, but perhaps more likely to do it on purpose.

Anya was scared, but she wasn't in shock. Most people went through life believing that nothing bad would ever happen to them. Anya had already faced disaster. Her whole world had ended, and yet she was still here, all these years later.

And she knew about kidnapping. Her parents were from a district in Russia where it was not uncommon. They never let her leave the house without her phone, and they always called—a call, not a text—if she was more than five minutes late home. They had already lost one daughter and they weren't taking any chances with the other. They even installed a location-tracking app on her phone, just in case. Anya wondered what the old man had done with it.

She heard him open a creaking metal door, the noise echoing in what she guessed was a large open space. Then he dragged her across a concrete floor, around some obstacles, and through another door into what sounded like a small room. He unlocked the cuff from around her ankle—but before she had time to hit him, he wrapped the cuff around something else and attached it to her other wrist. Now she was tied to what felt like a table leg.

Anya heard him shuffling away. "What do you want?" she demanded. But after a few seconds of silence, she realized he had left the room.

Anya wriggled around until she was lying on her back. If

she could lift the table leg, her cuff might slip out from under it. She braced her feet against the underside of the table and pushed. But the table didn't move at all.

Perhaps something heavy was stacked on top of it—something she could push off. She stood, bringing her hands higher. There was just enough slack in the chain for her to touch the edge of the tabletop, though her hands were still stuck behind her back. Her fingers bumped against something made of metal. It felt oily, like a piece of machinery.

"Ouch!" Something stabbed her fingertip. The machine had sharp bits. Very carefully, Anya fumbled her way around the edges of it. It felt like a table saw, bolted in place.

On a school excursion, Anya had visited one of the many tunnels that ran under Kelton from the coal-mining days. She had seen the thick wooden beams that propped up the ceilings. Maybe this saw had been used to cut some of them. Maybe there were tunnels beneath her feet. A way to escape.

Except she was still stuck to this table.

Anya pressed both feet against the wall and tried to drag the table instead. It wouldn't budge.

She slumped against the concrete floor. Her only other option was screaming for help again. But she had no reason to think that anyone but the kidnapper would hear her.

Something clicked elsewhere in the warehouse. A light switch? With her head covered, there was no way to tell.

In another room, a machine began to hum and whir. Then

there was a series of deafening bangs, like a hammer against a tin fence. The sounds were too evenly spaced for a human to be making them.

Every muscle tensed, Anya waited for the wall of sound to disappear. After a while, she realized it wasn't going to. The old man had switched on that machine to cover any other noises he might make. She would never hear him coming. Nor would she hear him leaving.

She was blind and deaf and completely alone. For the first time since her sister's funeral, Anya cried.

Through His Teeth

Who are you?" Jarli demanded. The clock on the wall suddenly seemed very loud. He felt like his heart was crawling up his throat. "What do you want?"

"You're going to tell the police that you didn't get a good look at me," the old man said. "You saw my truck headed north on the highway out of town. You don't remember the license plate. If they ask about Anya, tell them you saw her walking back toward the school."

The old man's voice was completely flat. He didn't sound worried about getting caught. How had he captured Anya?

"I don't know any Anya," Jarli said. Maybe the old man would let her go if he thought she wasn't Jarli's friend.

"Don't try that with me," the old man said. "I don't need an app to know when someone's not being truthful. Lie to me again, and she's dead. Is that clear?"

Jarli gripped the sides of the chair. It was like he was falling off a cliff all over again.

"Is that clear?" the old man asked again.

Jarli nodded, as though the man could see him. "Yes," he whispered.

"You're going to lock this phone and put it in your pocket—*without* ending the call. I'll be listening to everything you say. If you try to tell the cops about the phone, Anya dies. If you end the call, Anya dies. Understood?"

"But the police aren't going to believe me. If I had seen your truck headed out of town, why would I have run away and jumped off the cliffs?"

"Not my problem. *Make* them believe you. Once you leave the police station, I'll have more instructions."

The door opened. Constable Blanco stepped in, holding a plastic cup filled with water.

"Gotta go," Jarli said.

"Don't end the call," the old man warned.

Jarli locked the phone and put it in his pocket. He felt sick.

"Who was that?" Blanco asked.

Sweat formed on Jarli's brow. Whenever he watched a crime show or read a mystery novel, he always found himself wondering why the characters didn't tell the police what was going on. He should do that now.

But the old man could hear him. What if Jarli talked, and Anya died?

"Everything okay?" Blanco pressed.

Jarli could feel the old man listening.

"Fine, yeah," he heard himself say. "It was just my dad."

Blanco hesitated for just a moment. "Oh good," she said. "Is he on his way?"

"Um, no."

There was a pause.

"Mum's coming," Jarli added. He realized he was standing up, and he sat down again. "Can I go home soon?"

Blanco nodded. "You're not a suspect. This won't take long."

"I'm ready," Jarli said. But he'd never felt less ready in his life. What was he going to say?

"Okay. Bess already told us about the events in the gym. What happened after you broke the window in the infirmary?" She held up her hands, as if telling him to stop. "You're not in trouble for that—we just want to know what happened."

"Well . . ." Jarli's brain was going at a million miles per hour. "There were some kids at school who were angry about my app. Doug Hennessey and his friends. They'd gotten in trouble for lying and they blamed me."

"Did Doug say what the app had revealed about him?"

"No."

Blanco looked relieved. Jarli wondered why.

"So anyway," he said, "they were banging on the door of the gym, and there were no teachers around, so I had to break the window to—"

"Wait. *Kids* were banging on the door of the gym?"

Jarli nodded vigorously. "Yeah. I broke the window to escape and started running toward the bush to hide, but they saw me—"

"What about the old man? Bess said *he* was banging on the door—and then Anya chased after him when he left."

That explained how the old man had caught her. "Really?" Jarli said. "She must have gotten confused."

This time he heard the quiet beep from Blanco's phone.

She looked at Jarli. He looked at her.

She was using his app, he realized. She knew he was lying—she probably had all along. And now she knew that he knew that she knew! But if he told the truth, the old man would kill Anya.

Jarli's heart raced. He took a deep breath, trying to calm his nerves. The app could tell he was anxious.

"So the kids chased me up the hill—"

Beep.

"And they cornered me at the edge of the cliff—"

Beep.

"And then they charged, and I fell."

Beep.

"Then when I got out of the water, you found me," Jarli finished.

Blanco stared at him. Then she said, "What about the gun-shots?"

"Gunshots? I never heard any gunshots."

Beep. Jarli felt his cheeks grow hot.

Blanco said. "Bess told us that the old man—"

"The old man with the brown truck? Yeah, I saw him driving out of town this morning. He went north on the highway."

Beep.

Jarli blinked some sweat out of his eyes.

"Jarli," Blanco said, "you're lying."

"My app is still supposed to be in beta testing," Jarli said. "It has bugs. Like, when someone is nervous, it assumes they're lying."

This was pretty much the truth. No beep.

"Everyone heard gunshots," Blanco said. "Teachers, students—that's why the school called the police. You didn't hear them?"

Jarli shook his head, so her phone couldn't hear him lie.

"You're sure?"

She wasn't going to accept a silent answer. "I still can't hear very much," Jarli said, which was true. "I went right down to the bottom of the lake."

"You're not in any kind of trouble," Blanco said. "But without the truth, I can't help you."

Jarli swallowed. "If you're accusing me of something, I think I need a lawyer."

Blanco looked at him for a long time.

"Wait here," she said finally.

She stood up and walked out, closing the door behind her.

Jarli took the phone out of his pocket. A notification light blinked threateningly on the side, showing that there was an active call.

He put the phone to his ear. "This isn't working," he said. "She doesn't believe me."

The old man didn't sound impressed. "Did she lock the door?"

"I don't think so."

"Then leave."

"But she told me to stay."

"You'll have to sneak out."

Jarli couldn't believe his ears. "It's a police station. They'll notice."

"Sneak out, or Anya dies."

"Okay, okay. I'm doing it." Jarli stood up and hurried over to the door. He listened for a moment. It didn't sound like anyone was outside.

He pushed the door open a crack.

A police officer was standing right there. He peered through the gap at Jarli with cold gray eyes. Jarli got the feeling that Blanco had asked him to stand guard.

"Bathroom?" Jarli squeaked.

The officer pointed wordlessly.

"Thanks." Jarli slipped past him and walked quickly up the corridor. His mouth was dry. There were cameras in the ceiling. Maybe no one was watching him right now, but when

Blanco realized he was gone, it wouldn't take the police long to find him.

Jarli turned a corner and kept moving. The bathroom door was up ahead. He walked past it.

There was a fire exit at the other end of the corridor. A sign said: EMERGENCY USE ONLY—DOOR ALARMED. He couldn't go out that way. Not without getting the attention of every cop in the building. But it wasn't a dead end. There was another corner. Maybe it would lead him back to reception, or to another way out—

Blanco and Frink emerged from around the corner.

Jarli ducked back and pushed through the bathroom door. It fell shut behind him. His stomach churned. Had they seen him?

Other than the two cubicles and a trash can overflowing with paper towels, there was nowhere to hide in the bathroom. They would find him immediately. Jarli listened at the door, holding his breath.

"Why would he lawyer up if he hasn't done anything wrong?" Frink was asking.

"He's hiding something, for sure," Blanco replied. "But that doesn't mean . . ."

Her voice faded away to nothing. They hadn't seen him.

He opened the bathroom door a crack and peeked out. No one around. He walked toward the emergency exit and turned, going back the way Blanco had come. He found himself facing a row of offices with nameplates on the open doors and tinted glass around the doorframes. He walked past them, trying to look like he belonged here. Not easy for a kid in a police station, covered in mud. Fortunately, most of the offices were empty. The few cops at their desks didn't look up from their computers as he passed.

There was no sign of a way out. Jarli turned around and went back toward the bathrooms. He would have to sneak past the interview room, somehow, and get to the front entrance that way.

An alarm screamed.

Jarli almost leaped out of his skin. The noise hurt his ears and made it hard to think. Blanco and Frink must have realized the interview room and the bathroom were both empty. He had to get out of here right now. The old man's voice echoed through his head: *Sneak out, or Anya dies.*

Jarli ran toward the emergency exit and hit the crash bar with both hands. It opened with a clank and a scrape and then he was out in the daylight.

PART THREE: FUGITIVE

When telling the truth, people tend to include only the unexpected details—the things that surprised them at the time. A liar will include ordinary details, describing everyday things.

—From the documentation for Truth, *version 1.3*

On the Run

The parking lot was half full of police vehicles. There was a chain-link fence topped with barbed wire, but the gate was open. Jarli didn't see anyone guarding it. He sprinted across the asphalt, weaving around the police cars, and raced through the gap onto the busy street.

The reporters were still in front of the police station, but the alarm had distracted them. All eyes were on the main entrance, where bright lights were flashing and police officers were clomping down the steps. Were they surrounding the building, or evacuating? Jarli didn't know.

He ran past a thrift store, a supermarket, and a cafe, away from the commotion. He was looking for a crowd to blend into, but there was only one pedestrian around—a man in dark glasses and an expensive-looking fedora, carrying a newspaper. Jarli suddenly recognized him. It was Mr. Gorman.

Maybe he could help Jarli. Gorman used to work in private security. He and his bodyguards must have dealt with situations like this. Jarli opened his mouth to yell out to him—

And then realized that he couldn't. The old man was still

listening. Even if he got Gorman's attention, how would Jarli explain what was going on? If he tried, the old man would kill Anya.

After a moment, it was too late. Helpless, Jarli watched as Gorman climbed into a sports car—not the electric sedan he'd been driving last night—and zoomed off.

The police officers were trying to shoo the journalists away. Soon someone would see Jarli. He ducked into an alley and hid behind a sour-smelling Dumpster, pressing his back against the brick wall.

He lifted the phone to his ear and took a shaky breath. "I'm out."

"I know," the old man said. "I'm tracking the location of the phone. I know everywhere you go and everything you say."

Jarli suddenly wondered if his old phone had been tracked, too. That could be how the old man knew he was in the school gym earlier.

A sense of helplessness settled over Jarli. He had lied to the police, and then he had run from them. The old man had Anya, and he could hear everything Jarli said. What could Jarli do? He felt like he was going to throw up.

"Listen carefully," the old man said. Some kind of machine clanked ominously in the background.

"Please don't hurt Anya," Jarli begged. "I'll do whatever you want."

"Yes, you will. We're going to make a trade."

"What kind of trade?"

"You're going to go home. You're going to collect your father's laptop. Then you're going to bring it to me."

Jarli shut his eyes. This was a nightmare. "Our house was robbed," he said. "Someone stole the laptop."

"Not that one. I want his secret laptop."

"He doesn't have—"

"Yes, he does. It's in your house somewhere. You're going to find it and bring it to me. You have two hours."

Why would Jarli's dad have a secret laptop? The whole thing made no sense. "That's not enough time," Jarli said. "I don't have my bike—it'll take me an hour just to walk home."

"I've already booked a cab for you. It should be there any second."

Just as he said this, a car pulled up next to the alley. Jarli peeked around the edge of the Dumpster. It was a taxi, with Caroline behind the wheel.

"Don't hang up," the old man reminded him.

Jarli pocketed the phone and approached the taxi. Caroline's smile faded as she saw the mud on his clothes.

"Hey, Mrs. Deshara."

"Hi, Jarli. Don't get in yet."

Caroline got out of the car, pulled a towel out of the boot, and laid it across one of the back seats.

"Thanks," Jarli said, though he knew she hadn't done it for his benefit. He climbed in.

Bess was also sitting in the back. Her mum sometimes gave her a lift home when a fare took her near the school.

"Jarli!" she cried and hugged him. "You smell terrible."

"Good to see you, too," Jarli said.

"What happened?"

Jarli couldn't lie to Bess, especially not with Caroline's phone using *Truth Premium* to check everything he said. But with the old man listening, he couldn't tell her the truth. He wished he knew sign language.

"You know that cliff at the top of Weirwalla Hill?" he began. "Above the lake?"

Maybe Bess could help him. As he talked, Jarli got the phone out of his pocket. He thought maybe he could type a text message and show Bess the screen. Something like "help me." But the phone was locked, and Jarli didn't know the PIN.

"Well, I was looking for somewhere to hide . . ."

Still speaking, he held a finger to his lips, telling Bess to be silent. Then, with his fingertip, he drew three letters on the shiny glass screen of the phone: *SOS*.

He showed Bess the dirty smudges. She stared at him.

"But I ended up falling off the cliff," he said.

Caroline shook her head. "You're lucky to be alive. You know a guy broke his ankle jumping off there last year?"

Bess got out her own phone and typed a text message. She showed Jarli the screen.

What's going on?

Jarli took the phone from Bess and typed a message.

The old man is listening to us. This phone was waiting for me at the police station. He's using it to track my location. He has Anya. If I don't do what he says, he's going to kill her.

Bess's eyes widened. She took her phone back and started typing.

"Who broke his ankle?" Jarli asked Caroline. "Tell me all about it."

Caroline started rattling off everything she knew about the incident, giving Jarli the chance to check what Bess had written.

What can I do?

He borrowed the phone.

As soon as you drop me off, call the police and tell them what's happening.

Bess took the phone back.

You said this phone was waiting for you at the police station.

How do you know the police aren't involved?

Jarli felt his heart sink. She was right. The old man couldn't have brought the phone to the police station if he was guarding Anya somewhere else. He had someone working with him.

Unless—

Don't think about it, Jarli told himself. But the thought came anyway: *Unless Anya is already dead.*

A Losing Battle

Jarli took Bess's phone back and started typing.

Try to get through to Constable Blanco. The old man
didn't want me telling her anything, so she must be clean.

"Hey, Mum," Bess said aloud. "Can I hang out at Jarli's
place for a while?"

"Uh, sure," Caroline said. "If it's okay with Jarli's parents."

Jarli thought of the old man, listening to this. "I don't
know," he said. "I won't be staying long. I have to go out
again."

"Where are you going?" Caroline asked, sensing a potential fare.

Jarli didn't know where the old man was going to send him
once he had the laptop.

"Out jogging with Dad," he said.

Caroline's phone beeped. *Lie.*

Caroline grinned. "Secret boys' business, eh? Okay, fine. You don't have to tell me."

"It'll take ten minutes, tops," Bess said. "I just want to talk to you about my blog."

Jarli frowned. That made no sense. Then he realized what Bess was trying to do.

He borrowed her phone again.

You're a genius.

The car pulled up in front of the house. Jarli pulled his wallet out of his pocket. It was so encrusted with mud that it made a crunching sound when he opened it. He offered a dirty twenty-dollar bill to Caroline.

"You keep that," she said. "You paid the fare online when you booked the cab. Remember?"

The old man must have done that. Maybe the police could identify him from his credit card details. Then again, maybe he'd paid in untraceable bitcoin, or used the Supply Chain cryptocurrency.

"Oh right," Jarli said. "Well, see ya."

He and Bess clambered out of the cab. Bess hobbled around to the driver's side and gave Caroline a kiss through the window before she drove away.

When they got inside the house, no one else was home. Jarli found a note on the bench.

Jarli,

Hooper is sick. We're taking her to the emergency vet. Tried to phone you but couldn't get through.

Call me ASAP.

Love, Mum

Bess read the note quickly. "What's this?" She talked loudly for the old man's benefit. "Looks like your family is taking the dog to the vet. Your mum wants you to call her."

"I can't," Jarli said, equally loudly. "My phone died."

"Here, take mine. I'll be in the other room."

Bess handed over her phone, but she didn't leave the room. Jarli dialed Mum's number from memory. The old man would be able to hear everything he said, but not what Mum was saying. He hoped that was enough not to get him or Anya in trouble.

Mum picked up quickly. "Bess! Have you heard from Jarli?"

"It's me," Jarli said. "My phone died. How's Hooper?"

"I don't know. I found her convulsing and throwing up. At first I thought it might be a snakebite, but the vet couldn't find any tooth marks. He thinks she might have eaten something she shouldn't have. You didn't put any snail bait in the yard, did you?"

"No. Is she going to be okay?" Jarli found it hard to breathe. For a moment he forgot all about Anya and the old man. Hooper had been with his family since Jarli was six years old. They had grown up together. She couldn't die.

"The vet doesn't know. Where are you?"

"I'm at home."

"Well, call Caroline and get her to give you a lift here."

"I can't."

"It's okay—we'll pay her when you get here."

"I can't, Mum."

"Jarli," Mum said. "If you don't come now, you might not get another chance. Do you understand what I'm saying?"

She thought Hooper was dying. But Jarli couldn't sacrifice Anya's life, even to say good-bye to his dog.

"I can't," Jarli choked. "I'm sorry. I have to go."

He ended the call and handed the phone back to Bess who disappeared with it into his bedroom. Jarli grabbed a tissue to wipe away some tears and snot.

When he lifted the other phone to his ear, the old man sounded angry. "You're wasting time, Jarli."

"My mum and dad aren't here," Jarli said. "I'll find the laptop. Just give me some time to get rid of Bess."

"Be quick."

"I don't want to make her suspicious. She might call the police."

"You're a smart boy," the old man said. "You'll think of a way to make her leave. You have ten minutes."

Jarli pocketed the phone and ran into his bedroom. Bess had queued up the latest episode of Jarli's podcast—the one where he interviewed Bess.

"So what do you post on your blog?" a recording of Jarli was asking.

"I write about literature, mostly," recorded Bess said smoothly. She sounded much more formal when she had her interview voice on. "I take classic novels and compare them to their modern equivalents."

"For fun?" Recorded Jarli sounded skeptical.

Real-life Jarli left the old man's phone right next to Bess's, so he would think Jarli and Bess were having this conversation right now. Then he and Bess escaped back into the kitchen, out of range of the phone.

"This is full on," Bess hissed. "What should we do?"

"He wants Dad's laptop," Jarli whispered back.

"Didn't someone steal it?"

"He says there's another one, hidden somewhere in the house. I have to find it."

Bess looked doubtful. "Why would your dad have a secret laptop?"

"I dunno. Maybe he doesn't. The old man could have mixed him up with someone else. Maybe it's a company laptop, and Gorman was supposed to be the target. But if I can't find it, I don't know what I'm gonna do."

"If you bring it to him, do you think he will let Anya go?"

Jarli hesitated. "Why wouldn't he?"

"If this is about your dad, then he only came after you—*three times*—because you're a witness. Anya is a witness too.

She was at the scene of the car crash, and at the falls. And now she knows where his hideout is."

Jarli had a sinking feeling in his chest. "You think he's going to take the laptop and kill us both?"

"Maybe."

Bess might be right. But Jarli couldn't see another way out.

"Help me find the laptop," he said. "If it's not here, Anya's *definitely* in trouble."

They started the search in Mum and Dad's room. Jarli looked under the bed, in the wardrobe, and through every drawer. He found tissues, nail clippers, old magazines, and the creepy pillow that had been delivered this morning. No laptops. Bess helped him search, but her crutches made her slow.

Jarli could hear the podcast getting near the end in his bedroom. They were running out of time to talk openly.

"If the old man kills me—" he began.

"I'm not gonna let that happen," Bess said.

"Listen to me. If he does, you have to tell Mum and Dad what happened, okay? Tell them everything. I don't want them to think I just disappeared, or that I died in an accident." He remembered Mum's words: *Did you ever stop to think about what you were doing?* Tears stung his eyes. "I don't want Mum thinking that I just wasn't careful."

"Your parents aren't going to blame you for this," Bess

said, "and you're not going to die. Help me move this bookcase. Maybe the laptop is behind it."

Jarli grabbed one end, and they dragged the bookcase
away from the wall. A dictionary fell off the top and hit the
floor with a little explosion of dust. There was nothing behind
the bookshelf except cobwebs.

They had run out of places to search.

"Maybe he hid it in another room," Bess said.

"Maybe." But Jarli didn't hold out much hope. It was a
small house, and Dad couldn't have hidden the laptop in
another room without running the risk of someone finding it.

On autopilot, he picked up the dictionary to put it back on
the shelf—

And felt something shift *inside* it.

Jarli opened the dictionary. He had once wondered why
his father, who looked up everything online and hated cross-
words, had a physical dictionary. Now he knew. The pages
had been cut, creating a hollow. Inside was a small, thin laptop.

The old man had been right—but Jarli wasn't relieved.
What secrets had Dad been hiding?

"Let's see what's on it," Bess said.

"But the podcast is about to finish."

Bess snatched the laptop out of his hands. She opened it
and sat down on Mum and Dad's bed. "You go talk to the old
man," she said. "Stall him. What's your dad's birthday?"

"January third, 1977," Jarli said. "But Dad's a data-security engineer. He's not going to use his birthday as a password."

Bess typed it in. "I'm in."

"Huh," Jarli said. Maybe Dad *wanted* the laptop to be hacked.

Bess shooed him away. "Go, go!"

Jarli ran from the room and up the hall. He reached his bedroom and snatched up the phone just as the recorded version of Bess said, "Thanks for having me. Bye!"

Jarli closed the bedroom door loudly. Then he picked up the phone. "Okay," he said. "She's gone."

"You thought it was a good time for a ten-minute chat about literature?" the old man said.

"It worked, didn't it?" Jarli said. "She left. I'm looking for the laptop now."

"Look fast. If you're not here in eighty minutes, Anya dies."

"I'm doing my best! You don't need to keep threatening me."

"So far, your best isn't good enough." It was almost exactly what Mr. Kendrick used to say, and it left Jarli feeling just as helpless.

He ran back into his parents' room. Bess was staring at the laptop, eyes wide.

Jarli sat next to her on the bed so he could see the screen. Then his eyes grew wide too.

Dead Man's Switch

If you're reading this, I'm probably dead.

Don't be fooled into thinking that I just left Kelton.
They always make it look like the victim ran away, or
died in an accident. But I love my family and I would
never leave them. If I'm missing, I was murdered, plain
and simple.

You need to send all the files in this folder to the
media and the federal police. And not just one police
officer—as many as you can. I don't know how many
people are involved. I don't trust anyone, and neither
should you.

I work at CipherCrypt, which provides secure data
storage. It's our job to keep our clients' files safe from
criminals.

Now I know we failed.

Two weeks ago I was trying to fix a data
corruption problem in one of the servers when I
stumbled across a hidden file called VIPER. It was
just a list of names, and I would have ignored it

except that I recognized one of them: Hugo Niehls.

There had been a story about Hugo Niehls in the paper—he'd recently testified against a gangster he used to work for. The day after his court appearance, he vanished. The police couldn't find him. Everyone thought the gangster must have caught up with him somehow, but they could never prove it.

I checked the other names on the list. They were all people who had made powerful enemies. They were all missing, presumed dead. And they were all CipherCrypt clients.

Here's what I think happened. I think someone hacked us, and used our database to hunt these people down.

If they can get into CipherCrypt, they can get into anything. Your laptop. Your phone. Your car GPS. The computer that controls the plane you're flying in. Your pacemaker. Nothing is safe.

I don't know who wrote the VIPER file. Maybe the hacker left it behind by mistake. Ben Gorman found evidence that it came from India, but we can't narrow it down more than that. We would have taken all this to the police already, except we're not sure they can be trusted. And I'm afraid of what "Viper" will do to my family—whoever or whatever Viper is.

Below is the original file and all the other evidence I could find. Please, if you're reading this, do what I couldn't. Send it out to as many places as you can.

Then run.

Sincerely,

Glen Durras

P.S. Josie, I'm so sorry. I wish I'd picked a normal job, something that wouldn't have gotten me mixed up in this. Then we could have gotten old together, watching the kids grow up. They're lucky to have you. So was I. Please remind them often how much I loved them.

Bess got to the end of the note before Jarli did. She opened a new document and started typing.

We should do what he says. Send all these files to the cops, the media—everyone.

Jarli was still reeling. Dad's anxiety over the last few weeks made sense now. And the message on the pillow: *Rest in Peace, Jarli.* That might not have had anything to do with the app. The warning might have been intended for Dad, not Jarli.

He grabbed the laptop.

We can't. If the old man finds out, he'll kill Anya.

Bess opened her mouth and then closed it again. Jarli typed:

E-mail the files to yourself. If I don't come back
from the trade, then you can send it to the police.

I'm going with you.

You can't.

You need backup!

Jarli looked at the crutches, laying on the bed like cross-
bones. Bess glared at him.

YOU NEED ME!!!

Jarli lifted the phone to his ear. "I've found the laptop,"
he said.
"About time," the old man said.
"Where are we going to make the trade?"
"Listen carefully."

Showdown

Jarli's one-person bike was carrying two passengers. Footrests were mounted on either side of the back wheel for this purpose. He and Kirstie rode it together all the time. But Kirstie was smaller than Bess, and she had working legs to catch her if she fell off.

It was a bit wobbly, but Jarli focused on steering while Bess wrapped her arms around his chest and held on tight, his backpack and her crutches squashed between them. Luckily the journey was mostly downhill.

The sun crawled toward the horizon, racing them. Jarli pedaled furiously along the highway, his legs aching. Every jolt through the handlebars hurt his sore wrist. When this was all over, he wanted to lie down and sleep for about two days.

Assuming he survived. Whoever wrote the VIPER file seemed willing and able to make people vanish without a trace. When Mum, Dad, and Kirstie got home from the emergency vet, they might find Jarli missing—and then they'd never see him again.

Jarli should have left a note or something. He hadn't

thought of it—the old man hadn't given them much time to get to the warehouse.

And what about Caroline? What would she do if her daughter didn't come home? Jarli felt guilty for getting Bess involved in this. It had been her choice to come to the trade, but if Jarli hadn't told her what was happening, she would be safely home by now.

He wanted to apologize, but he couldn't. The old man was still listening, in his pocket. Jarli didn't want him to know that he had a passenger.

Cars and trucks zoomed past, so loud and close that the rushing air nearly knocked the bicycle over. If Jarli and Bess didn't come home tonight and the police started asking questions tomorrow, Jarli wondered if any of the drivers would remember seeing two teenagers on a bicycle. Probably not.

They rode past a gas station, a fast-food place, and the Big Canary—a tourist attraction that got hardly any tourists and even less maintenance. The giant statue's concrete feathers were stained with the poo of real birds. Then there was just mile after mile of withered bushland.

The green sign came before Jarli was ready for it.

KELTON EAST EXIT ¼ MILE

The trail was thirty feet beyond it, just like the old man had said. It was just wide enough for a car to drive through, and there were fresh tire tracks in the dust. Tall trees bent over the trail, dry branches creaking in the wind. The setting sun cast long shadows that could have concealed anything.

Jarli and Bess climbed off the bike. The old man hadn't said how far up the trail the warehouse was, only that it wasn't visible from the road. Jarli was supposed to knock on the door, alone. Then Anya would come out.

Bess had already typed a message on her phone. She showed Jarli.

I'll follow you from a safe distance. As soon as Anya is out of the warehouse, I'll e-mail your Dad's documents to the cops.

Jarli took the phone.

And if he doesn't let her out?

Bess took it back.

Then I'll come in and beat him up with my crutches.

Jarli forced a smile. This was a terrible time for jokes. Bess was typing again.

If you have to go inside, I'll wait for ten minutes, and then I'll make a distraction.

Like what?

Don't know. I'll think of something.

Thanks. Stay safe.

You too.

Jarli hopped back on the bike and rode carefully down the trail. The front wheel bumped and shuddered across the dirt. Screeching insects fell silent as Jarli rode past. He wondered if the old man would hear him coming. Maybe even now he was in the sights of a rifle.

He won't shoot me, Jarli reasoned. *At least not until he's sure I brought the laptop.*

He heard the warehouse before he saw it. A banging, grinding sound was coming from inside. Some kind of machine—the same one he'd heard on the phone. Jarli was amazed that the building even had power—when he spotted it through the trees, it looked like it had been abandoned years ago. No glass left in the windows. Parts of the wooden walls rotted away. Creeping vines carpeting the roof, camouflaging it. The building would have been invisible from the air.

The brown truck with the bull bar was parked nearby,

scraped paint from the crash obvious this close. Seeing it sent a spike of terror through Jarli's chest. He felt like he was spinning again, back in the car crash with Dad. He couldn't make his feet move.

Don't be a wuss, he told himself. *Anya's counting on you.*

He didn't know her very well. But he knew she hadn't frozen up when he needed her. She had helped him after the crash, warned him about the old man at the school, and followed him up to the cliff to see if he needed help.

Jarli forced himself to walk past the brown truck, then all the way down the hill toward a narrow door around the side of the warehouse. He knocked.

Nothing happened. He pulled out the cell phone to ask what was going on, but the machine noise made it impossible to hear if the old man was speaking.

Jarli raised his fist to pound on the door more loudly—

And then the door slowly creaked open.

Jarli backed away, but no one was standing there. The door had opened on electric hinges. Probably by remote. This building looked ancient, but someone must have made modifications very recently.

The rectangle of darkness beckoned to Jarli.

This wasn't the deal. He was supposed to knock, then Anya was supposed to come out. That was what the old man had said.

But no one seemed to be coming. And Jarli couldn't stand here all night.

Jarli took a deep breath, as if he was about to go underwater. Then he stepped into the warehouse.

The door slammed closed behind him.

Trap

Bess watched from the bushes at the top of the hill as Jarli disappeared into the warehouse.

"No, no!" she whispered. This wasn't how it was supposed to go. Anya was supposed to come out.

She pulled out her phone to call the police. But even if she could get through to Blanco without alerting the other officers, Bess didn't trust her to get here in time to save Jarli and Anya's lives.

Glen Durras's documents were on her phone. She could send them to the police *and* the media, just like he had asked. But if the bad guys realized she had done it, they might hurt Jarli and Anya. She should only do that as a last resort, if she was sure Jarli wasn't coming back out.

Bess had known that something would go wrong. Now, as usual, it was her job to get Jarli out of trouble.

He thought of her as the helpless one, she knew that. He didn't pity her like everyone else—he didn't assume that her life was a living nightmare, like some of the other kids did—but he still felt responsible for her. He never seemed to get that it was the other way around. He would be pretty much helpless without her, at least at school. Lots of people would be, come to think of it. Whenever there was a problem, it was always Bess coming up with good ideas—or gently talking people out of bad ones. And every time Jarli offended somebody by being too direct, Bess was always the one who made it okay. "When Jarli said baseball was boring," she had explained to a horrified classmate, "what he *meant* was that it has a slow pace. It's more suspenseful than other sports."

But she'd never had to rescue him from a kidnapper before. This was a new low.

She checked her watch. She had promised him a distraction. She had five minutes left to come up with one. But the noise from the warehouse was loud. Even if she screamed—which had been her plan—no one inside would notice. The old man would never hear her.

She could go down there and bang on the door with her crutch. But if the distraction worked, she wouldn't be able to run fast enough to get away. And Jarli wouldn't leave her behind, so they'd both be caught.

She had to come up with something else. Something loud enough to be heard, but far enough away to stay safe—and alarming enough to need the old man's attention.

She emerged from the bushes and hobbled toward the truck. A horn blast would probably do the trick. The old man might not even recognize the sound of his own horn—he might think someone else's car had arrived. Maybe even the police. But what if the truck was locked?

It won't be, Bess told herself. *It's parked in the middle of nowhere.*

She took the long way around, limping through the shrubbery, keeping as many trees as possible between her and the warehouse. She didn't see anyone, but couldn't shake the feeling that she wasn't alone. Was someone watching through those broken windows?

Hair standing on end, Bess stopped to peer into the shadows.

Then she spotted the other car, farther away, hidden behind some trees. It was an expensive-looking black sedan. Someone else was here! Jarli had walked into a trap. Bess took a deep breath. She had no choice but to go on.

She crept up to the truck.

"Please, please, please," she whispered.

She tried the handle. Locked. This far from town? Where was the trust?

She looked at the car window and hefted her crutch. Would she be able to break the glass?

Maybe. She could swing that crutch pretty hard. She had used it as a baseball bat once, when she'd been smoothing things over with the kid Jarli had offended.

A window smashing would make a lot of noise, especially if the car alarm went off. That might be even better than a horn. Bess gripped her crutch and waited. Ten minutes, she had told Jarli. He had been gone for seven. In three minutes she would upload the documents and make her distraction.

"Hello?" Jarli called out.

If anyone responded, he couldn't hear them over the machine.

"Anya?" he yelled louder.

Finally the machine switched off. The silence left Jarli's ears ringing.

As his eyes adjusted to the darkness, he saw that this must once have been a timber yard. Steel beams, like raised train tracks, lined the concrete floor where logs would once have been stacked. A rusted power sander stood on a rickety workbench. There was a big tool cupboard, currently closed. A generator was sputtering near the wall, filling the air with a faint stink of gasoline. Various types of saws hung on the walls. They looked like sharks' jaws, kept as trophies by fishermen. An open door led to what might have been an office.

He couldn't see Anya anywhere.

A light clicked on, blinding Jarli. He held one arm up in front of his face. It was like being on a stage. The spotlight somehow darkened the rest of the room.

Then he heard the old man's voice.

"Where's the laptop?"

It sounded like he was somewhere on the other side of the

room. His voice, rough and gravelly, was more frightening in person than on the phone.

"In my backpack," Jarli answered.

"Take out the laptop and put it on the floor, where I can see it."

Jarli hesitated. "But—"

"Do it!"

Slowly, Jarli did as he was told.

The old man spoke again. "Now, where's the girl?"

"I thought *you* had her," Jarli said. "That's why I'm here."

"Not Anya," the old man said. "The one with the crutches."

Jarli's heart beat a little faster. "You mean Bess? What about her?"

"You brought her with you."

"No I didn't."

A beep from the other side of the room. *Lie.* The old man had a *Truth* app installed.

Jarli squinted through the light. He could see a silhouette next to a closed door—the old man. And he wasn't alone. Another person stood in the shadows next to him, too tall to be Anya. Too broad across the shoulders.

"Where is Anya?" Jarli demanded, changing the subject.

The old man pointed at the closed door next to him. "Through there. But you don't get to see her unless you tell me where the other girl is."

"I don't know what you're talking about."

Another beep. *Lie.*

The other man spoke up. "There's no point lying to him, Jarli."

Jarli gasped. It was a familiar voice, yet his brain refused to recognize it.

But when the man stepped out of the shadows, Jarli couldn't deny the truth any longer.

"Where is Bess?" Mr. Gorman said.

Revealed

r. Gorman?" Jarli asked. "What are you doing here?"

"Just tell us where Bess is," Gorman said. His usual friendly smile was gone and his voice had a hard edge. He was standing perfectly still. In his tailored clothes, he looked like a store mannequin.

Jarli was desperate for a reasonable explanation. Maybe Gorman's car had broken down on the edge of the highway, and when he was walking back to town, he'd found the trail and followed it to the warehouse. Maybe he thought the old man was a cop or something. Or maybe he had been kidnapped, too.

Somewhere, deep inside his panic, Jarli knew that none of these ideas really made sense. What made more sense, seeing Gorman standing there, so serious, so commanding and sure . . . what terrified Jarli so much he couldn't even process it, was the idea that Gorman had *hired* the old man. Dad had told Gorman about the VIPER file—and Gorman had tried to have Dad killed.

"No one else needs to get hurt," Gorman said carefully.

"I know your father copied the VIPER file. I know that he bought a new laptop on his credit card, and I know that Cobra couldn't find it when he searched your house."

The old man—named Cobra, apparently—stared impassively at Jarli.

"I planted a listening device inside your home this morning," Gorman continued. "We're running a pretty complicated operation here, and I didn't want your dad to expose it. I needed to see if he knew that the car crash was an attempt on his life, and whether or not he'd warn his family. He didn't—but I overheard a conversation between you and Bess. I know you found the laptop and I know she got into it. My aerial drones followed her from your place to here, but they lost her on the dirt trail. So, where is she?"

"I don't know," Jarli insisted, his mind racing.

Beep. Jarli saw Gorman's phone screen flash orange: *Half truth.* Jarli didn't know exactly where Bess was, but he knew she was nearby.

"Once the evidence is gone," Gorman said, "it's just your father's word against mine. Why would I hurt Bess then? I just need to see if she has the files and if she sent them to anyone."

The app wasn't beeping, but Jarli still didn't trust Gorman. He knew now that his dad's boss was ruthless—he had made all the people in the VIPER file vanish, and then when Dad found out, Gorman sent Cobra after him. Jarli couldn't believe he hadn't worked it out earlier. Gorman was rich enough to hire a killer. He could access CipherCrypt's servers because he designed and owned them. Jarli had seen him hanging around the police station just after the old man's phone mysteriously turned up there. He had collected Jarli's family from the hospital—pretending to care, but really grilling them for details. He'd even provided chicken soup for Dad . . . which Hooper had eaten right before she had to be rushed to the emergency vet.

"You killed my dog!" Jarli screamed. He charged at Gorman. His anger made him feel like he had superstrength. He expected to crash into Gorman and send him flying across the room.

Cobra blocked Jarli with one outstretched arm. It was like hitting a steel bar. Jarli fell to the floor, wheezing, and definitely powerless. Cobra pinned him to the concrete, crushing Jarli's injured shoulder with a steel-capped boot.

"Tell me where Bess is, or Anya dies," Gorman snarled when Jarli had stopped coughing.

Jarli couldn't trade Anya's life for Bess's. "I don't know!" he cried.

The phone beeped again. Jarli knew the bad guys wouldn't believe him, but he couldn't think of anything else to say.

"For a smart kid, you're pretty stupid," Gorman said. "Let's see if you're willing to look Anya in the eye and tell her that she's going to die."

He gestured to Cobra, who hauled Jarli to his feet and

dragged him toward the closed door. Jarli tried to twist out of his grip, but it was impossible.

Gorman opened the door. "Bad news, Anya," he said. "Jarli has just decided . . ."

He trailed off.

Jarli saw that the room had nothing in it other than a workbench with a table saw on it. Under the saw was a puddle of metal splinters and a shredded handcuff.

Anya wasn't there.

Lurking

nya was in the tool closet, bleeding.

Given that she'd been using a table saw to cut through a handcuff attached her wrist—with her hands behind her back and a bag on her head—the cut on her hand wasn't too bad. Probably not even deep enough to need stitches. But it stung and the pain was distracting. Plus, she had left a trail of bright red drips, leading all the way from the workbench to the tool closet. Anyone looking down would see where she had gone.

She had hoped to get farther away—at least out of the building, and possibly all the way back to Kelton. But then Jarli had turned up. She couldn't leave him behind, so she'd stayed. Even though she had no idea how to get them both out alive.

It was pitch-black in the closet, and there was no room to move. The air smelled like dead mice. Hammers and saws hung from rusty hooks, poking into her back. If she moved, they would probably rattle. So she stayed still.

"Where is she?" a voice demanded. It was the guy Jarli had called Gorman.

"She was here a minute ago," the old man said. "She can't be far away."

"Well, find her! Now!"

Footsteps echoed through the workshop. It had sounded like Gorman was wearing running shoes. Cobra wore boots. Anya thought he was the one walking around.

"Run, Anya!" Jarli screamed.

There was a sharp slap, and he fell silent. Anya's heart raced.

She could hear Cobra lifting things, walking, pausing, walking some more. He was drawing closer and closer to the closet. She didn't think he'd spotted the blood yet. But he would look in here soon, one way or the other.

If Anya waited until he opened the closet door, she wouldn't be able to overpower him. There would be no room to move. But if she leaped out when he was too far away, he would see her coming. He might even have time to take a shot at her. She had to attack when he was exactly the right distance away.

The old man's footsteps drew closer. Anya took a deep breath, preparing all her muscles for a sudden explosion of force—

And then a phone chimed.

The sound seemed to come from the other side of the warehouse, where Anya thought Gorman was holding Jarli.

"Oh no!" Gorman said after a pause.

"What is it?" Cobra demanded.

Run, Jarli, Anya thought. *While he's distracted!*

"Viper sent me a message." Gorman's voice was shrill with panic. "He says someone just uploaded all Glen's evidence to social media."

"I'm gonna kill that girl," Cobra snarled.

Anya heard Jarli gasp. "No!"

"Viper says the press have already picked up the story," Gorman said. "They're demanding a statement from the police force. We're done for."

"I can't go back to prison," Cobra growled. "Not because of a bunch of idiot kids. We have to deal with them once and for all. Then Viper can get us out of here."

His last footsteps had sounded close to Anya's closet, but his voice was more distant, as though Cobra was facing the other way. *Now or never,* Anya told herself.

She burst out of the closet and charged.

Cobra reacted quickly. He whirled around and swung a hairy-knuckled fist at Anya. It was the sort of blow that would have knocked her down when she was a beginner boxer, but not now. She ducked under the punch and felt it skim the top of her head. The follow-through had shifted his whole body, and an instinctive, split-second calculation told Anya that he was about to put his weight on his right foot. So she kicked it out from under him.

The old man slipped over and hit the concrete, yelling

with rage. Anya spun around to face Gorman, expecting him to attack her.

He didn't. Instead, Gorman grabbed Jarli by the hair. His other hand pressed a sparkling blade to Jarli's throat.

"Don't move," he said.

Deep Cut

Jarli could feel the knife touching his skin. He didn't think it had drawn blood yet, but it felt sharp. He was even afraid to swallow.

Jarli hoped Anya had a plan. But it didn't look like it. She was motionless, feet shoulder-width apart, fists by her sides. She seemed to realize that any sudden movements could put that blade into Jarli's neck.

But doing nothing wasn't an option. Cobra had dropped his gun, but he would pick it up again in a second. Then the two kids would be at an even worse disadvantage.

Jarli did not consider himself an angry person, but right now he hated Gorman more than he'd ever hated anyone or anything. Jarli had just wanted to make an app. Anya was just a girl who had tried to help him. Dad was just a regular guy who wanted a normal job. Gorman had ruined all their lives.

"Don't move," Gorman said again.

Cobra was getting up behind Anya. "If he touches me," she told Gorman, "I'll put him right back down on the ground."

"No you won't," Gorman said. "You'll go with him to his car outside. Jarli's going to come with me."

"The cops already know everything," Jarli said, keeping his chin up to avoid the blade. "What's the point of taking us with you?"

"No talking," Gorman snapped. "Now, walk toward the door. Slowly. And don't—"

SMASH! The brown truck crashed through the walls, sending shards of wood flying. The bull bar knocked over the warehouse generator, spilling gasoline across the concrete floor. The front wheels slammed into one of the steel beams and the truck stopped with a colossal *thump*. The vehicle door swung open, and they had a clear view of the inside.

It was empty.

Bess watched from the top of the hill as the truck hit the warehouse, plunging through the wall like a bowling ball through a set of pins.

She had promised Jarli a distraction, and a speeding truck hitting the wall had seemed like a good one. Better than just honking the horn. But after she broke the window and released the hand brake, the truck rolled down the hill way too fast. She had expected it to hit the wall and stop, making a loud noise. Instead it shattered the wall and ended up inside the warehouse. She hoped Jarli and Anya hadn't been stand-ing near that wall.

Should have gone with screaming, she thought.

When she called the police, they had told her not to go into the warehouse. "Don't be a hero," the dispatch officer had said. "We'll be there soon. Don't do anything stupid." Bess wondered if crashing a car into the building counted as stupid.

Sirens wailed on the breeze. If Bess had heard them a minute earlier, she wouldn't have released the hand brake. She would have waited. Why weren't they coming quietly? Did they *want* the criminals to get away?

Maybe they were in on the whole thing, like Jarli's dad had suspected.

Bess hobbled back up the trail. She couldn't outrun the bad guys, so she needed a head start if they came this way. Her wrists and palms ached from the crutches. *Too much walking today.*

Something flashed between the trees. Headlights. A police car zoomed past without slowing down, tires growling along the dirt.

A second patrol car was right behind it. This time the driver saw Bess. The car stopped and the window rolled down. A woman with a chipped tooth was behind the wheel.

"You're Bess?" she said.

Bess nodded.

"I'm Constable Blanco," she said. "More officers are right behind me. We're going to surround the warehouse. You stay well back, behind the cordon."

"My friends are inside," Bess said. "Jarli and Anya."

Down the hill, the first patrol car had screeched to a halt next to the warehouse wall. A cop leaped out and ran toward the door. Another cop stayed near the car, his eyes on the hole in the wall. He held a megaphone to his lips.

"This is the Kelton Police Department," he bellowed. "The building is surrounded. Drop your weapons and come out with your hands up."

He was exaggerating, since only he and his partner had reached the warehouse so far. But technically they did have both exits covered. Bess wondered if Jarli's app would think he was lying.

"Don't worry," Constable Blanco told Bess. "We'll get your friends out. You just need to stay back, okay?"

Bess nodded.

Blanco drove down the hill toward the warehouse. A third car followed. Bess watched anxiously, cracking her knuckles. What if Jarli or Anya got caught in the cross fire between the kidnappers and the police?

There was nothing Bess could do other than stay out of the way, and hope. Feeling helpless, she hobbled back up the trail toward the road.

"Back!" one of the cops screamed. "Get back!"

Bess turned around in time to see the police scrambling away from the warehouse. A dim light flickered in the broken windows. She could hear a faint crackling sound. Smoke stung her nostrils.

"Fire!" Blanco shouted.

No Escape

When the truck crashed through the wall, Jarli took the chance to slip out of Gorman's loosened grasp. Recovering from his shock, Gorman tried to grab him again. Jarli darted out of reach, heart pounding, his eyes on the deadly blade.

Cobra reached down for the gun on the floor, but Anya was quicker. She kicked it across the room. It skated over the floor like a hockey puck on ice.

The four of them stood poised in a loose square, each waiting for the other to attack. Jarli felt the most vulnerable. Cobra was huge, Gorman had the knife, and Anya was apparently some kind of ninja. Jarli had nothing.

The stink of gasoline filled Jarli's nose. A puddle was spreading out from under the fallen generator. This place must have been abandoned years ago, but there was still sawdust on the floor. If the building caught fire, it would burn quickly. And after months without rain, the bush around it was ready to explode.

"Call out to Bess," Gorman said, pointing the knife at Jarli. "I know she's nearby. Tell her to come here."

"No," Jarli said.

A voice echoed from outside: "This is the Kelton Police Department. The building is surrounded. Drop your weapons and come out with your hands up."

Gorman and the old man looked at each other.

Jarli let out a breath he hadn't realized he was holding. They were saved!

"Better do what they say," Anya said. "If you wait for them to come in and get you, things could get ugly."

"They're not coming in." Cobra pulled a gold lighter out of his pocket. He opened it, and a flame danced inside, like a toy ballerina on a music box.

"What are you doing?!" Gorman shouted, alarmed.

"I'm not going back to prison," Cobra said, and he threw the lighter into the puddle of gasoline.

Flames spread over the surface of the puddle like a shock wave. There was a *whumpf* as half the air in the room was sucked into the hungry fire. The workshop had been dark before; now a dull orange glow cast shadows upward across the walls. The heat cooked Jarli's skin, but his insides were frozen with terror.

Fire. Everywhere. Jarli felt like a cornered animal. He was too scared even to think.

Anya grabbed his hand. "This way!" she hissed, and pulled him toward the hole the truck had made in the wall. Jarli kept his nose buried in the crook of his elbow as he stumbled through the workshop, trying not to inhale the smoke and fumes. His eyes were streaming.

They'd almost reached the spot where the brown truck had come to its crashing halt . . . when a tongue of flame shot across the floor toward the fallen generator.

"Down!" Anya cried, and threw herself down on the concrete.

Jarli copied her, just in time. The generator exploded with a deafening *bang*, sending pieces of hot metal flying in all directions. They clanged against the roof and rained down against the floor, splashing the burning gasoline everywhere.

A sizzling fragment landed on the back of Jarli's neck. He screamed and slapped at it with his hands. He got it off, but his fingers blistered where he had touched it. The spot on his neck felt suddenly cold, like a chip of ice was stuck there.

"You okay?" Anya asked.

Jarli dragged himself to his feet. "I'm okay."

But when he looked around, he saw that there was a lake of fire between them and the hole in the wall. He turned to the front door, but couldn't even see it through the flames.

Now there was no way out.

Down the Hatch

H elp us!" Jarli screamed. "Help!"

But it was not the fire department outside; it was the police. What could they do? *Arrest* the fire?

"Stay low," Anya said. "The smoke is more dangerous than the fire."

"We're trapped," Jarli rasped. His windpipe felt like it had been shredded.

"I know."

"We're going to die."

"I know." Anya had none of Bess's optimism.

"Where are Cobra and Gorman?"

Anya looked around. "I don't know."

All the walls were burning now. As the fire closed in, Jarli spun around, perplexed. Both criminals had vanished. They couldn't have reached the doors, and they couldn't have burned up already. They had simply disappeared.

Jarli paused amid the chaos. It was impossible for them to be gone. Unless . . .

His heart fluttered with hope as it dawned on him.

"Look for a hatch," he croaked. "Or a trapdoor. Anything!"

Anya crawled along the concrete floor, hands fumbling. Jarli wriggled in a different direction, toward where he had last seen Gorman. He squirmed as the heat started melting the rubber of his shoes. He ducked under some fallen debris, hoping there was something beneath.

While he felt around the floor, his mind raced. Cobra hadn't intended to die in the fire. A plan had been forming behind those tiny, menacing eyes. He had thrown the lighter down just to keep the cops out. To buy himself some time to get to his secret underground bunker, or—

Clunk. Jarli's hands had found something on the floor, right in the middle of the room. Something made of metal.

Jarli traced around the edges. There were hinges. A handle. Already warm to the touch.

"I found it!" he yelled. But the yell came out more like a whisper. He could barely breathe.

He stood up and waved his arms to get Anya's attention. "Anya! I found it!"

Anya didn't look up. She was lying facedown on the concrete, one arm outstretched, like a swimmer frozen in midstroke.

"No!" Terror squeezed Jarli's chest. He waded through the smoke toward her and rolled her over. Her eyes were closed.

"Anya!" he cried. "Wake up!"

She didn't respond.

It felt like they were drowning in smoke. Jarli tried to lift Anya, but she was too heavy—or maybe he was just too weak. Instead he grabbed her wrists and dragged her across the floor toward the trapdoor. Her shoulders would be sore when she woke. If she woke.

Smoke stinging his eyes, the fire creeping ever closer, Jarli turned the handle. He lifted the door—it felt as heavy as a dining table—to reveal a square of darkness. Sweet, cold air flowed out of the hole from deep underground. Metal rungs were built into the concrete on one side, stretching down into the gloom. Jarli had no idea how deep the hole was.

He climbed halfway in. With one hand and both feet on the rungs, he dragged Anya toward the hole. When she was close enough, he wrapped his arm around her waist and tried to lift her onto his shoulder like a firefighter.

But she was too heavy. When Jarli moved his foot onto a lower rung, his legs couldn't take the weight. The rungs slipped out of his hands. He and Anya tumbled backward into the dark.

Secret Network

THUD! Jarli hit the dirt hard, and Anya landed right on top of him.

All the air rushed out of Jarli's lungs at once, and he couldn't get it back in. Even after he rolled Anya off, it felt like his chest was being squashed by a safe or a pallet of bricks.

He turned his head to look at Anya. He could hardly see her—he could hardly see anything, it was so dark down here—but he thought her eyelids were fluttering.

Jarli tried to say her name, but he couldn't find the air.

Finally Anya opened her eyes. "Jarli?" she said, and then coughed wildly for a whole minute.

Jarli still couldn't speak, so he squeezed her outstretched hand. Some air was coming back into his lungs now. It was like a leaking tire, but in reverse. How did lungs work, anyway? If he survived this, he promised himself he'd find out.

When she was done convulsing, Anya sat up and spat on the floor. "Jarli," she wheezed. "You okay?"

"Can't breathe," Jarli gasped.

"Don't try. Just relax your chest. Let the air come and go as it pleases."

Jarli tried. But it was hard to relax when he was in so much pain.

"Imagine that you are floating," Anya said. "Whenever I am winded, that always works me."

"Happens . . . often?" Jarli gasped.

"Do not try to talk. Yes, it happens. Sometimes at the gym I take a punch to the chest. It is never fun."

Jarli closed his eyes and pictured himself in the ocean, floating on his back, the sun on his face. Eventually his diaphragm stopped spasming, and he could breathe again.

"I'm okay," he said.

Anya was looking around. "Where are we?"

"I don't know." Jarli sat up. He had expected to see some kind of doomsday shelter, full of canned food, batteries, and bottled water—and two killers.

But they weren't here. Because it wasn't a bunker.

It was a tunnel.

Ben Gorman hurried through the dark. He didn't dare slow down. If the firefighters arrived in time to put out the flames, it wouldn't take the police long to figure out where he had gone. They'd be right behind him.

But he didn't dare speed up, either. The low ceiling had crags and beams, ready to break his skull if he was careless.

And the floor was littered with rotted railway ties. Mine carts used to carry coal along these tunnels, before someone ripped out the rails. The walls were split by dark turnoffs, leading who knew where.

Cobra—Ben didn't know the old man's real name—was ahead of him, carrying a flashlight. The bouncing, swinging light was all Ben had to guide him.

Cobra had worked for Viper longer than Ben had. He'd said that this was part of a network of tunnels, some abandoned after the coal mining stopped, others newly built by Viper and a secret group of contractors. There were exits in dozens of secret locations. If you knew the tunnels, you could get from almost any part of Kelton to any other part without being seen.

But if you didn't know the tunnels, you could spend the rest of your life down here, wandering through the darkness, searching for a way out until you hit your head or fell down a hole or died of thirst.

So Ben stayed close to Cobra. Cobra knew the tunnels.

"How much farther?" Ben wheezed. He wasn't used to this kind of strain. He had a platinum membership at Kelton's only gym, but riding an exercise bike while watching TV was not the same as staggering through an abandoned mine shaft in a half stoop.

"Another hundred yards or so," Cobra said, turning another corner. "You struggling, rich boy?"

"I'm your boss," Ben snapped. "Show some respect."

"Viper pays my salary, not you," Cobra said. "You're the one who got us into this, and he's the one who'll get us out."

"How?" Ben asked, trying not to sound desperate. He had never met Viper, and didn't know much about his operation. Ben secured Viper's data, but he didn't read any of it. Until now, he hadn't wanted to know.

"You'll see," Cobra said. "As long as you keep up."

Ben gritted his teeth and kept running.

After three more turns and a trek up some steps, Cobra pointed out a ladder bolted to the wall. The rungs were so grimy that Ben would have walked right past without seeing it.

"This should be outside the police cordon," Cobra said. "Hopefully the fire hasn't reached that tinderbox of a town yet. Come on."

He climbed up the ladder, the flashlight a dull glow in his pocket.

Ben hurried up after him. The rungs were rough with rust. The muscles in his legs burned.

Above him, Cobra was opening another hatch. Ben could hear insect noise, and the distant crackling of flames. Cobra scrambled out into the moonlight. Ben followed.

They found themselves surrounded by trees, creaking and rustling. The hatch was half buried in the undergrowth—no one would ever find it unless they already knew it was there.

Cobra switched off the flashlight. Ben could hardly see anything in the dark. The burning warehouse flickered in the distance, surrounded by police. The fire would destroy all the evidence, including the two kids. With the bush so dry, it would spread to Kelton—that'd keep the cops busy for a while. Ben just hoped he could get out of town before then.

"The main trail is just over here," Cobra whispered, pointing.

"Then what?" Ben asked.

Something rustled in the bushes nearly. Cobra held up a hand, and Ben fell silent.

Nothing else happened. Only the distant shouts of police officers broke the silence. Cobra must have startled an animal. It was gone now.

"If we can get to the highway," Cobra said finally, "Viper will send someone to pick us up. Be ready to—"

He didn't get any further. Ben heard the impact as a metal crutch swung out of the bushes and broke Cobra's nose. He made a strangled cry and fell over backward into the scrub.

"They're over here!" a voice screamed.

Young. Female. Bess!

"Hey!" she yelled. "The bad guys are getting away!"

Footsteps crashed through the undergrowth toward Ben. The police were coming.

"I see him!" another voice yelled. "This way!"

Ben could feel the net tightening around him. The police

were closing in. His heart making a rapid drumbeat in his chest, he scrambled back toward the hatch and lifted the lid. Without even thinking, he jumped back onto the ladder, pulled the hatch shut above his head, and dropped down to the tunnel below.

Without Cobra's flashlight, the tunnel was pitch-black. Ben ran, his hands outstretched in front of his face to protect his head from any hidden obstacles. His terrified breaths echoed around the stone walls.

When the panic subsided, he realized he was headed back to the burning building, which was also surrounded by police officers. Bad idea.

His fumbling hands found a hidden side corridor, and he entered it. Maybe he could find another exit. Somewhere closer to the rest of Kelton. He had getaway cars stashed in several rented garages around town. Each had fifteen thousand dollars in the glove compartment, along with a forged passport. If he could get to them before Cobra told the cops who he was, then he'd be able to get out of the state, or even the country.

After three more turns, his escape through the maze no longer seemed like a good idea. There seemed to be hundreds of tunnels, all so twisted that it was impossible to maintain his sense of direction. Especially in the dark. Ben reached for his phone, which had a flashlight app on it. Then he remembered that he didn't have it. He had left it in the warehouse, in case the police were tracking it. The fire would have destroyed it by now.

Ben decided to go back to the hatch near the trail. He could wait underneath it until the cops went away. They might not find the hatch, and even if they did, Ben could hide in the tunnels until they gave up. They couldn't search the whole network of mine shafts and corridors. It would take years.

Ben reached a fork in the tunnel and stopped. Which way led back to the hatch? Left or right?

Left, he was pretty sure. He turned and kept walking. But a few yards farther along there was a bend he didn't remember. Had he gone the wrong way?

The panic came back, stronger now. He didn't know the way.

It felt like the blackness was eating him alive.

"I surrender!" he shouted. The cops would take him to jail, but that was better than being lost down here in the dark.

His voice echoed around the web of tunnels, bouncing back a little quieter each time until it was gone.

"I give up!" he yelled, his voice going high and squeaky. "I want to come out!"

No one answered. Nobody could hear him. He couldn't find his way back to the hatch or the burning warehouse. He was lost. Alone. In the darkness.

Somewhere in the Dark

D id you hear that?" Jarli asked.

"Hear what?" Anya asked.

"Sounded like someone screaming."

Anya peered into the shadowy tunnel. "I heard nothing."

Jarli laid back down. "Maybe I imagined it."

They had decided to stay here, at the bottom of the ladder. The trapdoor stood open above them. They couldn't go back up because of the fire, but they weren't willing to follow the tunnel. Not with the bad guys lurking somewhere in the dark.

"What if the fire spreads down here?" Jarli asked.

"It won't," Anya said. "Heat goes up, not down. And all the gasoline would have burned up by now."

Jarli wished he shared her confidence. The crackling of flames had become a roar above them. It sounded like the world was ending. He hoped Bess made it to safety before the fire spread.

"So what were Cobra and Gorman actually doing?" Anya asked.

"Making people disappear. For money."

"Yes, but how? Where did they put their victims?"

"Dad didn't seem to know." Jarli stared into the gloomy mine shaft. "Maybe in these tunnels."

Anya shivered. "We will find out when the police search them, I guess."

They fell silent for a while.

"I have been thinking about your app," Anya said finally. "It will probably help more people than it hurts, but I do not think you should use it too much."

"Why not?" Jarli asked.

"Because if you trust too much, you will sometimes be hurt," Anya said. "But if you trust not enough, you will hurt other people. Soon you will find yourself alone. Trust is more important than truth."

Jarli considered this. Anya seemed like a good person. He owed her his life.

"Do you have secrets?" he asked. "Things the app might expose?"

"I do," Anya said. "But I won't tell you what they are. In fact, I will lie to you to protect them. It is my hope that you will trust me anyway—that you will believe that I mean no one any harm, and that I am your friend."

"Okay." Jarli extended his hand. Anya shook it. Then she tilted her head to one side, just like Hooper did when she heard a possum.

"Listen," she said.

"I don't hear—" Jarli began. Then there was a *boom*, like a distant explosion.

He gasped as something landed on his head. Something tiny and cold.

Another droplet landed on his palm. A hissing sound filled the air. Black spots appeared on the floor all around him, faster and faster.

It was raining.

After the Storm

ooper!" Jarli cried.

The dog ran up to him, wagging her tail and grinning. If she still felt sick after the stomach pump, she showed no sign of it. Like always, she just looked delighted to see him.

Jarli hugged her fiercely. "Who's my good dog? Who's the best dog in the whole wide world?"

Hooper woofed.

"You!" Jarli said. "That's right!"

"Normally we don't allow dogs in the station, unless they're guide dogs," Constable Frink said with a smile. "So if anyone asks, you're blind."

"Hooper was the victim of a crime," Mum said. "She has a right to be here."

"I assume someone will take her statement shortly?" Bess asked Frink, keeping a straight face.

"On paper, she's probably evidence," Kirstie said thoughtfully.

The police station felt much less scary than the last time

Jarli was here. Maybe that was because Cobra was handcuffed and locked up in a cell downstairs. Or perhaps it was
because Jarli was sitting between Anya and Bess. Being surrounded by friends and family made him feel invincible. And
the rainstorm, which had extinguished the fire and saved the
town, made him feel like his run of bad luck might be over.

Constable Blanco was interviewing Dad in the next room.
Dad had a lawyer with him, but Jarli didn't think he was in
trouble. He wasn't suspected of any crime, other than not
contacting the police sooner. Blanco had said he wouldn't be
charged for that, given that he had feared for his family's lives.

Now that Jarli had discovered Dad's darkest fears, he
hoped that they could finally be honest with each other. Dad
shouldn't have to worry alone, and Jarli should know when he
was in danger.

But he remembered Anya's words: *Trust is more important than truth.*

Mum and Kirstie were sitting opposite, quizzing Anya.
Mum kept asking boring, polite questions, such as: "And what
do your parents do, Anya?" Jarli noticed Anya's answers were
vague, especially when it came to her father.

Kirstie seemed to be in awe of Anya. Her questions were
more like, "Can you do a backflip?" and "Is it true that the
Russian government has captured a UFO?" and "Could you
kill someone with both hands tied behind your back?"

"Kirstie!" Mum said. "That's a horrible question to ask."

"I never tried," Anya told Kirstie. She sounded serious, but Jarli thought he could see a smile hovering at the corner of her mouth.

"Cooool," Kirstie whispered.

Dad emerged from the interview room with Constable Blanco and the lawyer. Dad looked exhausted. Unlike Jarli, he'd been unraveling this conspiracy for weeks. Retelling the whole story must have been hard.

"Dad!" Jarli cried. He ran up and hugged his father. Dad squeezed him tightly.

"I'm so glad you didn't get hurt," Dad said. "I'm sorry I got you mixed up in this."

"It's okay, Dad. Everything's okay. It's over."

Kirstie got there a second later, and then Mum wrapped her arms around everybody. Jarli had so many questions, but he didn't want to spoil the moment.

"Glad you're all right, Mr. D," Bess said when everyone had let go.

"Thanks," Dad said. "And thank you for looking after Jarli."

Bess shrugged, but she looked pleased. "I always do. At least this time Anya did most of the heavy lifting."

"Jarli," Constable Blanco said. "I'd like to talk to you, next."

She gestured to the open door of the interview room. Jarli wondered if he was in trouble.

"It's not too late to correct some of the things you told me last time," Blanco added.

Mum and Dad raised their eyebrows.

"Uh, okay," Jarli said. "Sure."

He followed Blanco in. She gestured for him to shut the door behind him.

"First, congratulations on your courage during the last twenty-four hours," Blanco said. "Your quick thinking probably saved Anya's life."

"Have you found Mr. Gorman?" Jarli asked.

"Still no sign of him. But we have almost the whole force looking. Pictures of him have been distributed all over the country. And we found the listening devices."

"Listening devices?"

"The one in your home. One was inside the vacuum flask, where we also found traces of the poison your dog ingested. The other was sewn into a pillow, with 'Rest in Peace, Jarli' written on the top. We think Gorman wanted to know if your dad suspected him personally, so he sent the pillow to provoke a conversation he could then listen to. It wasn't a bad plan—he wouldn't even have needed to come back to steal the evidence. Your family would have gotten rid of both listening devices within a week."

"But the pillow was mailed days ago. How did Gorman know my app was going to go viral?"

"That's another question we'd like to ask him," Blanco said.

"What about his victims?" Jarli asked. "Did you find them?"

Blanco frowned. "His victims?"

"I read the message on Dad's secret laptop," Jarli said. "Mr. Gorman and the old man—and maybe someone else— they were making people disappear."

"Yes," Constable Blanco said. "But they weren't victims. They were clients."

"I don't understand," Jarli said.

"They were very rich people who had made very powerful enemies. So they paid a crime lord—code-named 'Viper'— to help them vanish. Mr. Gorman was laundering the money for Viper. Clients would pay him, supposedly to secure their data, and he would give the money to Viper. I don't know who Viper is, or how he was helping these people escape, but Ben Gorman will tell us . . . when we catch him."

It all made sense now. "What about the old man?" Jarli asked. "Cobra. Couldn't he tell you how the whole thing worked?"

"Maybe," Blanco said. "But so far, he hasn't said a word. He hasn't even asked for a lawyer."

"Who is he?"

"We don't know. Nothing in his pockets, no labels on his clothes. No hits on the facial recognition database. His finger- prints have been burned off. We're waiting on a judge to give us permission to take a blood sample for DNA. Whoever he is, I think he's been doing this a long, long time."

"He said he'd been in prison," Jarli said.

"Really?" Blanco scribbled a note to herself. "Must not be

a local prison, or we'd have him on file. Did he have any kind of accent?'"

"I don't think so." Jarli leaned back in his chair. He wondered what would have happened differently if he hadn't made the app. Maybe he would have figured things out faster, because he wouldn't have assumed that Cobra's attack was anything to do with him. Or maybe Gorman would have been able to hurt Jarli's family more easily, because they wouldn't have been surrounded by reporters all the time. Or perhaps everything would have ended up exactly the same.

"Can I ask you something?" he said.

"Sure."

The door burst open. It was Constable Frink.

"Blanco," he said. His eyes were wide.

"I'm in the middle of an interview," Blanco said.

"It's Cobra," Frink said. "He's gone."

Not Over

Constable Blanco didn't stop Jarli from following them downstairs to the cells. If Cobra was loose in the building, Jarli didn't want to be left alone.

There were four cells, bars painted white, scratches on the mirrors, the brickwork worn but solid. A TV was positioned so that all the cells could see it. A news report was playing silently on the screen.

All four cells were empty. But one of them had a folded piece of paper lying on the ground.

"He was right here," Frink was babbling. "He was handcuffed. The cage was locked. I was watching the stairs."

Blanco walked into the cell. She stomped on the floor, checking that it was solid, even though she must have been here many times before. She ran her hands along the walls.

"You're sure this was the right cell?" she said.

"I'm not an idiot," Frink said. "And the other cells are empty too."

Blanco pulled on a latex glove and picked up the piece of paper. A name was written on one side:

Jarli

Blanco read the other side, her eyes growing wider and wider.

"We searched him," Frink said. "He didn't have anything to write with."

"He didn't write this," Blanco said.

"What does it say?" Jarli demanded.

Blanco showed it to him.

This time, I'll let you and your family walk away. But don't interfere with my work again. Cobra was one of many, and as you can see, nowhere is safe. The next time I strike, you won't see me coming.

—Viper

ACKNOWLEDGMENTS

Thank you to the eagle-eyed team at Simon & Schuster for taking a chance on this book and refining it for North American readers. Thanks to Scholastic Australia for inviting me to write the series in the first place. Thanks to all the readers, librarians, booksellers, teachers, and parents who made *Liars* a hit. Thanks to Curtis Brown Australia, as always, for helping me navigate the world of publishing. And thanks to my family and friends for somehow keeping me afloat and grounded at the same time.